GALLOWS
FOR A
GUNMAN

<u>BOOK YOUR PLACE ON OUR WEBSITE</u>
<u>AND MAKE THE</u>
<u>READING CONNECTION!</u>

We've created a customized website just for our very special readers, where you can get the inside scoop on everything that's going on with Zebra, Pinnacle and Kensington books.

When you come online, you'll have the exciting opportunity to:

- View covers of upcoming books

- Read sample chapters

- Learn about our future publishing schedule (listed by publication month *and author*)

- Find out when your favorite authors will be visiting a city near you

- Search for and order backlist books from our online catalog

- Check out author bios and background information

- Send e-mail to your favorite authors

- Meet the Kensington staff online

- Join us in weekly chats with authors, readers and other guests

- Get writing guidelines

- AND MUCH MORE!

Visit our website at
http://www.kensingtonbooks.com

GALLOWS FOR A GUNMAN

ROD MILLER

PINNACLE BOOKS
Kensington Publishing Corp.
http://www.kensingtonbooks.com

For all my author friends around The Campfire—if they weren't so darn helpful, hanging would be too good for them.

LILA

Harlow Mackelprang's last supper was seasoned with my spit.

Truth be told, every meal he has eaten these past three weeks while confined in the town jail awaiting his appointment with the hangman has been adulterated at my hand. The trays that left this kitchen with a dish towel covering my disgusting sauces are small comfort given what that so-and-so did to me. But at least it's something—some revenge, however puny, for the years and months Harlow Mackelprang has sentenced me to stand on swollen ankles cooking in this café.

I should say right out that his is the only food I have ever tampered with. The very thought of such a breach of trust turns my stomach. But as I say, the man had it coming. And the fact that he got it pleases me even more than the knowledge that he will hang come morning.

Before Harlow Mackelprang went berserk, I lived an easier life. At least it seemed easier, as it was of my own choosing. The family home was four or five miles south of Los Santos. We lived just at the edge of lonesome, far enough from other folks to feel the isolation, but near enough to town that company was readily at hand.

My late husband Soren had watered that small farm with his sweat for nine years, including the six we were man and wife. I worked alongside him in the fields as much as housekeeping would allow. As the children came along my outdoors work, naturally, came second, and I spent my days with the usual routine of diapers and dishes, meals and mending, laundry and lap-sitting that every mother knows.

But that was when we had Soren to provide. That was before Harlow Mackelprang showed up at our door.

It happened on an early summer night three long years ago. The hour was late, well past the time most folks were abed, and the only people abroad in the land were likely up to no good. Soren had worked in the cornfield long into the moonlight, pulling and hoeing weeds whose only purpose on earth was to choke honest crops to death.

Soren and I talked quietly at the kitchen table as he wolfed down a late supper I had kept warm on the back of the stove. These late evenings, with the little ones asleep, provided longed-for opportunities for togetherness.

"I think now the weeds will give us no more problems," Soren said. "If we can keep it watered well enough, I believe the corn will give us a good crop. But still, we will be lucky to see it 'knee-high by the Fourth of July,' as the old saying says we should."

"How are the cows?"

"Well. The calves are growing quickly," he said, then paused to fork up another load of fried spuds and onions.

"The feed is holding up well, so the mothers are content. They have all they need to make the milk. Things will be fine as long as the stream flows."

A long draft of cool milk from a crockery mug prompted another interruption.

"In a month or so it will be time again for Odin to visit the cows."

For my late husband, that was about as direct a reference to the reproductive process as one would ever hear. I could not resist giggling. Soren could not resist blushing. Odin, you see, was our herd bull—or, as Soren would say in his prim and proper way, "our gentleman cow."

Sometimes, the fact that such a shy man had managed to father three babies in this farmhouse surprised me. Intimacy did not come easy to him, and talk of such things was a rarity.

But sire them he did, and Soren doted on our little ones. Grace was four then, and she was Momma's little helper around the house and barnyard, but Papa's girl nonetheless. Karl, our oldest boy, was barely twenty-two months, and enjoyed nothing more than his brief forays into the fields and pastures with Papa. Nothing made the boy happier or caused him to laugh louder than to ride horseback in front of Soren, propped on the saddle swells with his stubby legs wrapped around the saddle horn. Oscar was our baby. Just three months old, he demanded near-constant attention and my work those days had to conform to his schedule.

All three were tucked away and sleeping, as I said, giving us some quiet time that was too soon interrupted by an outburst of barking from our dog.

"What on earth could that be setting him off?"

"Or who, at this hour."

"I hear a horse coming. And coming fast. I guess we will know soon enough," Soren said as he rose from the table.

By the time he opened the door, the horse was already sliding to a stop in the dooryard.

"Who is it? Who is there?"

"It's me, Harlow Mackelprang," the rider said between gasps for air. But if he was winded, his mount was even more so. As it stood trembling in the patch of pale light that fell to the ground through the open door, I could see the horse was lathered and struggling for breath. The poor animal must have been raced at top speed every step of the five miles from town, where Harlow Mackelprang lived. The man's desperation was plain.

"What is it you want?" said Soren as I crossed the room to stand behind him.

"There's been some trouble in town. I gotta get away for a while and I'm a gonna need your help. Then I'll be gone."

"We're poor folks with little enough to see to our own needs," I said, hesitant to have anything to do with the man.

"You hush up, woman. I'll do my talking to Soren."

"You will not speak disrespectfully to my wife. Besides, what she has said is true. We have nothing to offer you."

We heard the click of the cocking hammer before seeing the pistol come up.

"Well, I'm taking what I want whether you're offering or not."

Harlow Mackelprang swung his right leg across the front of the saddle and over the horse's neck, never taking his eyes off us or even blinking as he slid to the ground. He dropped the reins and backed us into the room with his pointed pistol as he walked through the door.

"Let's start in the kitchen. Sack me up some flour."

"All we have just now is cornmeal," I told him. "Won't have flour until we go to town on Saturday."

"Sack it up. And tie up a bundle of salt. And pull down a string of them dried apricots there on the wall."

When that was done, he demanded a supply of coffee. Then he pulled my frying pan off its hook and picked up the coffeepot, the dregs of which he dumped in the wood box, clanking the upside-down pot against the side of the stove.

"Please. The children are asleep."

"Shut up. I know you got a root cellar. Let's go."

He waved us toward the door with his pistol, as if Soren and I didn't know the way out of our own house. As we crossed the yard, I tried to summon up what I knew of Harlow Mackelprang.

I first laid eyes on him some six years before that fateful night, and the first I saw of him was the holey soles of his run-down boots. It was my first day in Los Santos, and the morning had been an eventful one. Soren had met my train, escorted me to the justice of the peace to seal our vows, then treated me to dinner at the very café where I now cook. Then we loaded my trunk into the buckboard for the trip to the farm, and were just under way.

As we rounded the corner from Railroad Street onto First Avenue, a dog set to yelping and yowling to beat the band. The ruckus emanated from beneath the porch of a mercantile store, out from under which porch poked the aforementioned boots. Adding to the din was a wailing girl around ten years old, sitting in front of the store on an empty packing box.

Folks were gathering, and Soren stopped the

wagon as the apron-wrapped storekeeper dashed out onto the porch.

"What the Sam Hill's goin' on?" the storekeeper asked.

"Daddy! Harlow Mackelprang's hitting Sparky with a stick!" the girl told him.

About that time, a tall, stocky man with a badge pinned to his vest limped onto the scene, grabbed hold of those boots by the ankles, and dragged a boy out from under the porch.

Harlow Mackelprang stood up and dusted himself off, casting nasty looks by turns at the girl and her father and the lawman, as if undecided who most deserved his hate. He was a tall boy, taller than the storekeeper and nearly as tall as the marshal, with a pimply face and greasy hair.

It did not appear that he had dirtied bathwater for quite some time. Nor had his clothes been laundered of late. They were old, ill-fitting, and oft-patched, though not often enough to mend all the holes. His age was difficult to discern, what with him being so tall, but he must have been fourteen or fifteen years old at the time.

"What do you think you're doing, beating that dog?" said the marshal.

"Sonofabitch bit me!" the boy said, displaying a bloody scratch on the back of his hand.

"Nonsense!" the storekeeper said. "That mutt has been tied to this porch all day every day since he was a pup and he never so much as barks at anybody."

"He was teasing him," the little girl said. "He kept on poking him with a stick and boxing his ears, and so Sparky bit him. Served him right!"

"That so?" the marshal asked the kid, whose only reply was a defiant stare.

"You go on," the storekeeper told the boy. "Get away from here, and stay away. Picking on a tethered dog! What the hell's wrong with you anyway? Go on! Git! I don't want you or your sticky fingers around here."

"Better get along, boy," the lawman added. "Try to keep your nose clean."

Harlow Mackelprang shuffled off down the street, hands in his pockets and head down, casting more of those nasty looks back over his shoulder. He turned down the first alley that presented itself and was gone. Soren clucked up the team and we went on home for our wedding night.

Living out of town like we did those next six years, I didn't know much about Harlow Mackelprang's activities, except to say that whenever I visited with folks in town there always seemed to be a story in circulation about some mischief he'd been into.

And the older he got, the meaner he became, and the trouble he caused was of a more serious nature. But until that night, I never would have guessed how bad the man—even then barely more than a boy—had become.

I held the lantern while Soren laid back the door of the root cellar. It being small, with room for only one man and him unable to stand upright, Harlow Mackelprang handed Soren the fry pan and coffeepot.

"Don't do something stupid," he said, and stepped down into the cellar. He popped back up almost immediately, eyeing us with suspicion. In the instant, he had managed to snag a gunnysack with maybe seven or eight pounds of spuds left in the bottom. He shoved it toward Soren.

"Put that cooking stuff in there, and that grub from the house. How about meat?"

"There is the smokehouse," Soren said, nodding his head toward the small building.

Our guest climbed the four steps out of the cellar, then backed his way to the smokehouse and through the door. He soon handed Soren a slab of bacon and the butt-end of a ham we had been whittling on to add to the sack.

We were directed back across the yard toward the ground-tied horse, and I was relieved that Harlow Mackelprang would soon mount up and be on his way. Instead, he untied the latigo, pulled it through the cinch ring, and stripped the saddle. He then un-bridled the horse and sent it clattering off into the dark with a lash of the bridle reins across the hip.

"Leave them supplies here with the saddle and let's go catch me a horse."

"A horse!?" Soren said, incredulous, barely able to stifle a laugh. "You mean old Babe?"

"Babe? I ain't riding out of here on no mare."

"I should hope not. Babe is too old for getaways. Besides, she is my only horse and must serve for riding to work the cattle as well as pulling my farm implements and the buckboard."

"A mare. And a plow horse to boot. Damn the luck. Well, let's get her saddled. Bad as she is, she'll beat walking."

"No. You cannot have Babe."

"Don't make me ask again," the village-bully-turned-desperado said as he raised his pistol to arm's length, leaving but a foot or two between the muzzle and Soren's forehead.

Looking back, I suppose it's likely that my Soren felt no fear. He was a big man, tall and strong. His arms were the size of my thighs and his hands exactly as long as the small of my back was wide. Remembering the feel of his hands there can still kindle a warmth in me.

On celebration days in town when men got up to boys' games like wrestling, Soren more often than not would be the last man standing. He would strip his shirt for the contests to save the scarce fabric from rips and tears. The ropy muscles across his bare back, firm chest, and stomach, and his sculpted arms, always drew admiring looks from the circled men.

And, of course, more than a few lingering looks from the clucking coveys of womenfolk who pretended to ignore such childish games but were unable to keep their eyes averted for any length of time. Truth be told, the fairer sex is every bit as attracted to watching strong men grapple as the men themselves are. The reason behind the fascination may be different, but there it is.

So as I said, my Soren must not have taken seriously the threat Harlow Mackelprang represented. At least not seriously enough. Even with the cold, dark eye of the pistol barrel looking straight at him, Soren would not, or could not, see anything to fear in the sniveling beanpole standing before him.

"I said don't make me ask again!" Harlow Mackelprang screeched across the few feet that separated him from my husband, who stood calmly, his eyes following the nervous sways and dips of the pistol.

"It will do no good to ask. Babe is more important to this farm than even I. Without her, we have nothing. The horse goes nowhere."

Harlow Mackelprang did not reply for what seemed an eternity.

Then, without saying another word, he pulled the trigger and my husband's head exploded. Soren was upended by the blast and dropped to the ground as bits of scalp, skull, blood, and brain rained down around him. I watched, too stunned to scream or even draw breath.

As powder smoke drifted away in the deafening silence that followed the blast, I heard the baby crying as if in the faraway distance.

"We'll just see about that, you stupid Scandahoovian," Harlow Mackelprang finally said. "Now, woman, go get that horse or that squawking kid'll be next."

I did not bother to fetch a halter or catch-rope from the barn. Through the fog of shock I made my way to the corral gate, and lifted the iron ring that once held together the staves of a small molasses keg but now served as a gate latch. The ring swung from the end of its gatepost tether as I hefted the end of the pole panel and swung it a few feet away from the corral and into the barnyard.

Babe, while a bit fidgety from all the unaccustomed nighttime noise, did not object when I grabbed a handful of mane and tugged her to and through the open gate. She pivoted with me when I turned back to drag and lift the gate in place. Can't have the milch cow wandering off, I managed to remember through the daze surrounding me.

The ring clanged when I dropped it over the top of the post, and the horse snorted and shuffled backward a few steps. My clutching again at her mane calmed her, and I towed the old mare back toward the house and Harlow Mackelprang.

My baby's wails, weaker now and turning into hopeless sobs, carried across the thick dark air.

That murdering maniac was as twitchy and restless as I was dazed. Headstall already in hand, he slung an arm around the old horse's neck and jammed the bit against her poor worn teeth. Babe took the bit and he slid the bridle over her ears, not bothering to straighten and smooth the horse's forelock as my Soren would have done.

Upset at the unaccustomed jerking and yanking, the usually docile old horse threw up her head and shied sideways. Harlow Mackelprang yanked at the reins and Babe whinnied and scuttled backward, hind end practically dragging and her head thrashing from side to side. The impatient man wrenched her to a stop and lashed her across the face with the end of the leather reins.

"Stand still, you sorry sonofabitch!"

"There's no need to mistreat that animal," I said.

"You shut up. You ain't nothing but a woman. I'll deal with this horse a man's way."

"Soren never raised a hand to that horse in all the years he's owned him."

"Yeah, and what did being such a gentle sort get that big dumb bastard? Dead, that's what!" he squawked, throwing the saddle over old Babe's back.

Without bothering to straighten the skirts, free the whangs, or twist the kinks out of the latigo straps, he tugged the cinch snug. For good measure, but no good reason in Babe's case, he kicked her hard in the belly to make sure she wasn't swelled up with breath like some mounts would be to relieve the discomfort of a too-tight girth.

Tying off the cinch knot, swinging into the saddle, jerking the horse's head around, whipping her across the hips with the loose ends of the reins, raking her flanks with his boot heels, Harlow Mackelprang rode away from the ruins of my life at a dead run.

Come morning, the marshal and a posse showed up

inquiring as to the whereabouts of Harlow Mackelprang. Marshal limped along behind me around the yard as I led him through the events of the night before. He became more and more agitated as the reality of what happened here sank in, then apologized for seeming to wait so long to take up the pursuit.

But, he explained, first of all, all hands had been needed in town to extinguish a fire; second, their reasons for chasing the villain up till now did not rise to the level of murder; and third, he had not even imagined that the criminal would commit such a foul deed as that which he had done here.

Marshal held little hope of finding the trail, but did not hesitate in the attempt. He was kind enough to leave two men behind to dig a grave and help me lay Soren to rest. They recounted the events in town that occasioned the formation of the posse, but given the state of affairs and my state of mind, I couldn't really take in what they told me just then.

It seems Harlow Mackelprang had single-handedly executed a brief but vicious reign of terror in Los Santos. He beat up a soiled dove, shot and wounded a cardplayer he accused of cheating, then shot up the saloon for good measure, then set fire to the livery stable after stealing a getaway horse.

His deeds were so far removed from his usual cowardly bullying and petty thievery that folks were taken by surprise at the violent outburst. I imagined they would be even more surprised to learn he had gunned down a kind and gentle man like my Soren out of mere meanness.

There was no way, of course, I could keep the farm after that. The work it required was far beyond the ability of a woman with three babies to take care of. And since no one else wanted the farm, I could get nothing for it. The crops withered and the cows wandered off, there being no ready market for them and no way to keep track of the small herd until an opportunity to sell might present itself.

It so happened the café needed a cook and I needed some means of providing for my young ones, and the situation seemed as good as any, besides being the only one available. So Costello, the man who owned and ran the place, hired me on. I imposed on some of the town folk to haul my few belongings from the farm to an abandoned cabin at the edge of town, which made a small but suitable home for my family.

Neither Soren nor I had any kin in these parts. All our relatives were back in Freeman County, Minnesota, where we had both lived until Soren emigrated, with the understanding that he would send for me once established elsewhere. Not having the help of a mother or aunts or cousins, I arranged to pay a small sum to a woman to tend my kids. Her children were grown and gone and her husband spent most of his time off prospecting, and Mrs. Barlow was pleased with the proposition.

She turned out to be a godsend and the children are thriving in her care. I have precious little time available for them—a stolen hour or two here and there between meals. They seem to grow a little more every day in my absence, and sometimes I marvel that they are my own, as they often seem so strange to me.

Anyway, for these past three years I have carried the smell of hot cooking fat on my person. I have felt the tickle of trickling sweat as I stand over stove and sink and block, cutting and slicing and stirring and scrubbing and baking and frying and boiling. I have been sentenced to prepare three square meals a day for however many hungry patrons show up here, the length of the sentence being indeterminate and with no end in sight.

And yet, until his recent arrest and trial, the gunman who is the reason for my being here and Soren being in his grave has wandered free.

I have had neither the time nor the inclination to follow his exploits in detail, but I am aware that for these past three years Harlow Mackelprang has robbed and plundered and murdered throughout the region, always eluding capture.

Upon leaving our farm, they say he rode south and threw in with a gang of border bandits, and took over leadership of the group by ruthlessly murdering his rivals. His life of crime caught up with him, though, and tomorrow he pays the price. His sentence is death, and it will be served. My sentence, however, will go on—perhaps for life.

It is not the life I imagined. But it is the life I have, and I must make the best of it. Today, the best of it came after the supper rush, when I was called upon to prepare Harlow Mackelprang's last supper.

I sliced a steak from a joint of meat, and pounded it flat with an empty whiskey bottle kept by for that purpose. I rubbed the tenderized beef with salt and sprinkled it with flour and dropped it into a cast-iron skillet to fry in hot fat.

I dredged a generous serving of sauerkraut from the barrel into a saucepan and set it on the stove to heat, crumbling in a bit of leftover breakfast sausage.

This being a special occasion, I cut the lid off a can of peaches, drained off the excess syrup, and dumped the yellow slices into a china bowl. Earlier today I had set aside a portion of biscuit batter in anticipation, and I now stretched it to cover the bowl, pierced it with the point of a knife, and sprinkled it with cinnamon and brown sugar, then slid the small cobbler into a slow oven.

The gravy was gone, having all been served up on the many supper platters that went out by the pass-through window this evening. So after turning the meat, I poured some of the drippings into a smaller skillet and tossed in a handful of flour. Stirring the flour as it browned in the fat, I ladled in milk and slid the pan to a hotter part of the stove and kept on stirring as it came to a boil and congealed. Satisfied with its consistency, I added a sprinkle of ground pepper and set it aside to stay warm.

I splashed in a dollop of cream and a dipper of water and revived the mashed potatoes with a little stirring.

The bean pot was never allowed to empty, so all I had to do was give it a good stir, smashing some of the firmer beans against the side to thicken the mixture, then break up and stir in a dried red chili pepper.

I split three biscuits and smeared them with bacon grease, which the prisoner preferred over butter.

With all in readiness, it was time to prepare the plate. I selected a large china platter. A man deserves hearty portions for his last supper.

First, the steak. It covered more than half the plate, even though I left it hanging over the end and sides. Below and to the left, a generous serving of mashed potatoes. Beside it, a similar quantity of beans. And at the bottom of the plate, a steaming heap of kraut.

Before ladling gravy over the meat and potatoes I cleared my throat and added the final ingredient. Other unmentionables garnished the sauerkraut and seasoned the beans.

I pulled the cobbler from the oven and adorned it likewise before spooning on heavy cream. I poured a cup of scalding hot coffee and stirred in a small measure of liquid I shan't name along with a spoonful of sugar.

Finally, I placed the platter, the cobbler, the biscuits, and the coffee on a tray and covered all with a clean dish towel.

Then I carried the tray to the pass-through window from the kitchen to the dining room and handed it off to my employer Costello, who slid it across the counter and into the care of the deputy, whose job it is to carry it to the jail.

Tomorrow morning the café will be abandoned for the hanging.

I will leave my stove temporarily untended to witness the occasion.

I will work my way through the crowd to stand near the gallows steps, where I can catch Harlow Mackelprang's eye as he climbs to his death.

Perhaps he will wonder why I smile.

CHARLIE

Harlow Mackelprang's last supper was not as hot as it might have been.

Earlier this evening, I sat at a table at the café having coffee when it came out of Lila's kitchen and was placed on the counter on a neatly covered tray. I probably should have left my cup unfinished and delivered it to him as hot and fresh as possible.

Instead, I took my time. I'll be damned if I'll put myself out, then or now, just to make life more pleasant for a low-down murdering crook. Especially one that'll be dangling from the end of a rope before the world sees another sunset.

So I sipped my steaming Arbuckle's sweetened with sugar, and wondered at why Lila seemed in such a good mood as I passed the time with old man Costello standing behind the counter.

"Seems a shame to waste such a fine meal on a man like Harlow Mackelprang," I said.

Costello kept up with tracing patterns in a little scatter of salt he'd spread on the counter.

"Maybe."

He smoothed out the salt with the palm of his hand and took up tracing another pattern in it.

"But the price of a meal is the price of a meal so far as I am concerned. It matters not to me if the money comes from the county coffers or from the pocket of some drifting cowboy. So long as I get my price, it is all the same to me."

"I guess that's one way of seeing it."

Costello asked, "Is there another?"

"Well, a saddle tramp likely worked for the money that's feeding him. Even a cardsharp has to turn a few pasteboards to get fed. But Harlow Mackelprang didn't do a damn thing to earn the money it's taking to fill his belly."

"Still, it costs the same when I need to buy supplies or to pay Lila."

"But some of that money came out of your pocket, Costello! Some of it's mine. Every man in Los Santos shelled out his share of the money that's been feeding that damn thieving murderer."

"That is so. At least I am getting a little of mine back."

"That strike you as being fair?"

"Fair?" Costello said, swiping the salt from the counter onto the floor and brushing the palms of his hands together to rid them of the last of it.

"What is fair? Is it fair for me to feed your marshal more meals than he ever has or ever will pay for? This is not a public service I am running here. The pennies I get back for fixing meals for the gunman Harlow Mackelprang or whoever else you have locked up over there are small recompense for the dollars I have watched go down the marshal's gullet.

And how about you, Charlie? When was the last time you paid for coffee?"

At that, I figured I'd kept the prisoner waiting long enough, so I gathered up the tray and toted it over to the jailhouse to Harlow Mackelprang.

"Here's your supper, you ingrate," I told him as I slid the tray under the cell door. "And thank God it's the last time you'll be sponging off the taxpaying citizens of Los Santos."

"I ain't none too worried about that. They gave me nothing but a hard time my whole life. A slice of beefsteak won't hurt 'em none."

"You're damn lucky it ain't beans and biscuits like all the others who get locked up in here get. You could at least appreciate it."

That got a laugh out of him. "Appreciate it?" he snorted. "Hell, Charlie, I'm getting hung in the morning. Oughtn't I at least have the right to die with a decent meal in my belly?"

"What about Soren and Calvin and all them others you killed? They die with full stomachs? I don't suppose you cared a hoot in hell about that before you shot them."

"I'll have to think on that one. Let me see. As I recollect, Soren was sitting at the supper table when I showed up at his place," he said with a sneer. "I don't know if his belly was full, but he was sure working on it."

The heat climbed up my neck and I could feel my face burning red. I could barely control the rage quaking in my limbs enough to say, "Harlow Mackelprang, you are one mean sonofabitch."

"I reckon you're right, kid. And I hope folks never

forget it. At least I'll be remembered for something."

I went through the door into the office and told the marshal his prisoner had been fed. He sent me home for my own supper and told me to come back later for night duty. I knew Becky wouldn't be too happy about me sitting around the jailhouse all night instead of keeping her warm in bed. But the fact is, standing watch is part of the job, and the truth is, the only time we do it is when someone particularly nasty is locked up, which ain't often and she knows it.

Becky and me both have lived in Los Santos all our lives. Her dad kept the mercantile and my folks worked for the railroad, selling passenger tickets and keeping track of freight coming through the express office. So we have both known Harlow Mackelprang all our lives.

Being a few years younger than him, we were sometimes targets of his abuse and bullying. Of course that was true for most every kid. He especially had it in for Becky on account of she got him in trouble one time for tormenting her dog. She couldn't never prove Harlow Mackelprang did it, but someone hit that dog Sparky in the head with a hatchet shortly after. Like I said, no one could prove who did it, but everyone knew who did.

We married, me and Rebecca, just four months ago. Some folks—her dad especially—thought we should wait, us not being quite twenty years old yet, but we could not see any reason to wait. She wasn't going anywhere and neither was I, and nothing in Los Santos was likely to change either.

Besides, with her helping out around her dad's

store and me getting this deputy job, we figured we had the means to set up housekeeping. Lots of others hereabouts have gotten hitched with a lot fewer prospects.

Becky's folks and my ma and dad chipped in to help buy us a house, for which we owe a mortgage to the bank but we will pay it off before too long, we hope. It ain't as nice as what our folks have, of course, but it's fine for now.

For the sum of six hundred dollars we got title to a small lot just two blocks off Front Street down First Avenue. The house on it is a solid-built one of square timber with a shake roof. Becky says it's nothing more than an old log cabin, which is so, but it's a good one and has been kept up and fixed up by previous owners over the years. Besides, she's fixed it up right nice inside, I think as I step through the front door.

Becky didn't see me coming as she was standing over the stove. She turned when the door closed, and by then I had her around the waist and hoisted her up for a big old kiss.

"Charlie! Put me down," she said. "Can't you see I'm busy fixing your supper?"

"I see that. But I see something I want more than I want supper."

"You are incorrigible!"

"Is that what they call it? I've heard lots of names for what I'm feeling but that ain't one of them."

"Don't be silly. 'Incorrigible' means you're persistent and can't be discouraged. You'd know that had you paid attention to your lessons in school instead of scheming how you could steal a kiss."

"You got to admit that kissing always was more enjoyable than studying grammar."

"I don't have to admit any such thing. Now sit down at the table and I'll serve your plate."

Supper was a slab of ham with sliced and fried potatoes, and a hunk of cheese. I even got dessert, which was stewed apples and raisins poured over a slice of cake Becky had baked on the weekend for Sunday dinner, and which she had been rationing out ever since. Which, I guess, was a good thing or I'd have eaten the whole thing by Monday. I'll tell you, my Becky is a fine cook and makes even plain fare right tasty.

"Harlow Mackelprang," I told her between bites, "is having a steak dinner over to the jail right now."

"Jealous?"

"No, I'll take your cooking anytime. But I gotta say that beefsteak and gravy sure smelled fine. Seems a shame to waste it on a bum who'll be dead before the taste is out of his mouth."

"Hanging is too good for the likes of him," Becky said. "Harlow Mackelprang had the devil in him from the time he was a boy. I, for one, was not surprised when he advanced from tormenting people to murdering them. I will enjoy seeing him dead— and watching him die. I fully intend to be present at the hanging."

"Why, Becky, I did not know you had such strong sentiments about the man."

She did not reply right away, but from the way she was attacking that cake with a kitchen knife, I could tell she was stirred up. Finally, she said, "Charlie, you know he was a trial to this town all his life. He pilfered a small fortune from daddy's store, and then there was that time he killed my little dog Sparky. And you know how he used to pester kids at school."

"That's true enough. But I don't remember it being all one-sided."

"Whatever do you mean?"

"Didn't you tell me once how you and your dad shortchanged him on stuff at the store? You know, like putting a little thumb on the scale along with his flour sack and stuff like that?"

"Well, sure, but he stole lots more than that! We only tried to even things up a little."

"I don't suppose it ever occurred to you that you weren't really hurting Harlow Mackelprang with that kind of thing as much as you were old Broom."

"That old drunkard! He wouldn't know the difference."

"That's right. And that makes it all the worse."

"I don't want to talk about this anymore, Charlie. You're no innocent yourself. I'll never forget how you crept behind his chair that one time at a schoolhouse dance and cut the twine holding up his oversized hand-me-down britches. When he stood up and they fell down, it practically embarrassed that poor awkward boy near to death.

"Or when you and the other boys tipped the school outhouse over on him and left him out there in the cold for the better part of the morning. If he hadn't managed to kick enough boards out of the seat to crawl out through the bottom, he'd probably be in there yet."

"Yeah, I reckon them things and the others I done was mean of me. That ain't no way to treat Harlow Mackelprang or anybody else. I shouldn't have done them."

"So, since when did you become such a chum of Harlow Mackelprang's, concerned for his feelings and all?"

"Becky, you know as well as I do I have no use for him. Fact is, I was sorely tempted just this evening to pee in his coffee cup."

For some reason that struck Becky's funny bone, and she had a giggle fit that went on for some time. "Watch your mouth, Charlie! I can't believe a husband of mine could think such things, let alone speak of them in mixed company!" She was trying to sound prudish and straitlaced, but her laughter would not allow it.

"You ain't mixed company. You're my wife—the light of my life, my one heart's desire, the flame on my candle—"

"Do hush up. I know what's on your mind."

"You're a mind reader then, sweet Rebecca?"

"It's no trouble where you're concerned. You've only had one thing on your mind since we married. Before that too, I suspect."

The silly smile I could feel all over my face held my only reply.

"Besides, don't you have night duty at the jail?"

"It'll wait. Harlow Mackelprang ain't going anywhere."

Marshal was a tad bit aggravated that I took longer getting back than he expected. But it ain't like he was going to miss out on anything. I suspected his evening would go about as usual—cadge a free meal at the café and a few drinks at the saloon before falling into bed for several hours of uninterrupted snoring. The only thing that made this night any different was the fact that he'd have to get up a little early to supervise the hanging come morning.

"Hell's fire, Charlie, you forget you had a job to come to?" he asked before I had even cleared the front door.

"No, Marshal. Sorry I'm late. Becky had a little something extra special for dessert tonight."

"Hmmph. When you gonna get over being a newlywed and start into complaining about your wife like all the rest of us married men do?"

"I can't say as I've ever heard you complain about your wife, Marshal. That subject hardly ever comes up."

"Oh, I ain't got nothing to complain about really. It's just one of them things men do, you know. Sort of an unwritten rule like the Code of the West or something. You'll catch on eventually."

"I reckon I will. Whyn't you go on ahead and lock up and be on your way. I'll take care of things till morning."

Standard procedure in the marshal's jail at night called for bolting and locking the heavy hardwood panel door between the office and the cells. Once the bolt was shot and a heavy padlock hooked through the hasp, that door was about as secure as a bank vault. It would take a big batch of blasting powder to move it, and any attempts at it with a battering ram would raise enough noise to wake the dead. With it latched, we could both spend nights at home in bed and not worry about jailbreaks and such.

But with a crazy killer like Harlow Mackelprang locked up, we not only locked the door, but kept someone on night watch too. Most times that was me, but from time to time Marshal would recruit some other responsible man for a shift. Besides that, in the present situation the marshal was about as worried about folks breaking *into* the jail as he was about our star prisoner breaking out. More than a few loud-mouths leaning against a bar had allowed that they'd as soon get up a necktie party and string up the condemned as wait for it to happen all proper and legal-like. But with the hanging now within spitting distance, it wasn't likely that any angry citizens would try anything. At least no one who claimed to be on the right side of the law.

"Different deal tonight, Charlie," the marshal said without getting up or showing any sign of leaving. "I ain't locking the door, at least for now. There'll be some folks coming by who have business with Harlow Mackelprang, so it'll be easier just to leave it open. You'll have to stay awake and mind what's going on. I don't think there'll be trouble, but you never know."

"Who's coming by?"

"The preacher asked if he could come by. I told him it wouldn't do no good on account of Harlow Mackelprang being void of religion, but he figures it's his duty anyway and I never found no profit in arguing with a churchman, so I told him to come on ahead. That hangman the judge sent for, fellow name of Henker, will be around too."

"He will? What for?"

"Damned if I know. Something about sizing up the condemned, he said. Wants to make sure he gets the rope the right length for a clean hanging. I'll say this—the man knows his business. He's been all over that old gallows checking things out and or-dering modifications and adjustments. Tied a sandbag to his rope and dropped it through the trap a bunch of times to stretch all the give out of it and to check the workings of the door. The man seems downright fond of hanging. Fond of whiskey too. Takes a pull on a bottle every time he pulls that trip lever, and he's pulled it a goodly number of times."

"I don't see the point, Marshal. You haven't hung all that many men, but they're all dead. Whyn't the judge want you hanging Harlow Mackelprang?"

"I suppose it's on account of all the publicity. With a famous bad man like Harlow Mackelprang at the end of the rope, I think the judge just wants to make certain it all goes well. Don't want a sloppy hanging when there's so many folks watching. Anyhow, just let the hangman in when he comes and help him out if he asks."

"Yes, sir. Anyone else I should look out for?"

"Not that I know of. Them two Mexicans and that old man are still hanging around the saloon. I'm convinced they're the ones been riding with Harlow Mackelprang, so I suppose we should worry about them trying to bust him out, but I don't think they'll try anything. One of them came by here yesterday, and the old man was just here a while ago. He slipped Harlow Mackelprang a whiskey flask, but that's all."

"And you let him!?" I asked, surprised that Marshal would allow any such breach of security, him usually being a stickler for procedures—part of his being a military man.

"I didn't see much harm. Hell, the man'll be dead soon. I figured a drink or two might keep him in a better mood. Anybody else shows up, use your best judgment. Just make sure Harlow Mackelprang is still in that cell come the morning. Oh, and make sure he's still alive so we can kill him all legal and proper-like."

"You think someone might try to kill him?"

"Nah. By this time most folks are content to let the law do it. Keeps 'em from getting their own hands bloody. But anything could happen, so stay sharp."

"I'll do it, Marshal. Don't you worry."

"I'll be in before first light to make sure everything's in order come time for the hanging. Charlie, I'll want you to stay on until afterward. I want both of us armed to the teeth to march Harlow Mackelprang to the gallows."

"But I thought you weren't expecting trouble."

"I'm not. But a show of force never hurts. Just in case."

"I'll be here. This'll be my first hanging, you know. In an official capacity, that is."

"I know it, Charlie, and I hope it's your last. Mine too. I haven't had to stretch too many necks since coming to Los Santos, and I hope I don't have to stretch another." With that, he strapped on his gun belt and left. I wondered if he would sleep tonight.

I looked in on the prisoners just to satisfy myself that everything back there was as it should be. Harlow Mackelprang was laying on his cot like he hadn't a care in the world, his supper tray shoved into the corner. That whiskey flask the marshal talked about was nowhere in sight. Judging from appearances, he'd probably already drained the thing and stuffed the empty under the flea-infested tick that passes for a mattress in these cells.

Down in the end cell, the confidence man we had locked up while he awaited trial was sitting on his cot reading one of them Bibles he hawked. For such a windbag, Sweeney had been pretty quiet while locked up in here. Once he got wound up, it took him a while to run down, but like I say, he hadn't yapped too much.

Satisfied that all was well, I went back out to the office to relax and maybe steal a little shut-eye. That, as it turned out, would prove pretty much impossible.

I had barely settled in behind the desk when through the office door came a man I did not know. He was a heavyset man, with what was left of his hair trimmed so short as to be almost missing. Had a long, scraggly mustache dangling down. He was outfitted in a raggedy suit of clothes the likes of which a banker might have worn in its better days.

"What can I do for you, sir?" I asked.

"My name is Henker, boy. I believe you're expecting me. I have come to see Harlow Mackelprang," he said with a Dutch accent of some sort.

"That's right. Marshal said you'd be coming around. Anything I can do to help you?"

"Not particularly. I will not be long. I just wish to make some measurements and talk with the boy."

"Sure. Just out of curiosity, Mr. . . ."

"Henker."

"Henker, sorry. What is it you need to know and why?"

"What is your name?"

"Just call me Charlie."

"Yes. Charlie. Are you interested in snapping necks, Charlie?"

"Well, sir, I can't rightly say. I seen a few hangings here in Los Santos, but the marshal took care of those. I'm just wondering how someone like you can make someone like Harlow Mackelprang any deader. No offense, you understand."

"No offense taken, Charlie." He laughed and fished a bottle out of the pocket of his suit coat and pulled off a long swallow before continuing on.

"Hanging, you see, can be a terrible business if not performed properly. It is a matter of simple physics— get the drop right and the condemned is sent to hell in an instant with a broken neck. Figure it wrong, and one of two things can happen. Too short the drop, and the hanged man strangles, flopping around and kicking, dying slow and ugly. Too long the drop, and you can tear a man's head clean off his body with all manner of blood and gore. Either way, you can see, is most unsatisfactory."

"Yeah, I see what you mean. Them things ever happen to you?"

"Oh, yes. But not for a good long time. I learned from my mistakes. I am not as careful as some with my weights and measures, but I've a good eye and guarantee a good result."

"Well, there won't be anybody crying over your hanging Harlow Mackelprang, whether you do it up good or bad. Long as he's dead, folks'll be pleased. He's right through there, Mr. Henker. C'mon, I'll show you."

I made the introductions and propped myself in the doorway while Henker questioned Harlow Mackelprang quietly. I couldn't really hear much of what they said, except for a few horse laughs Henker let loose, and I didn't pay much attention. After a while, Henker motioned the prisoner closer to the barred door, then reached through the bars to grab Harlow Mackelprang by the throat.

"Hey there!" I said, instantly upright. "What's going on?"

"Don't worry, kid," Harlow Mackelprang said. "He's just fitting me out for a noose. This cold-blooded sonofabitch will choke the life out of me with a rope, not his bare hands."

"Thank you," Henker said to him as he withdrew his hands. "I believe I now know all I need to know to snap your neck. I shall see you in the morning. For the last time. And I shall be interested to see if you can take your hanging like a man." With that, he left Harlow Mackelprang standing in his cell and we passed back through to the office.

"Had me worried for a minute there," I said.

"I am sorry, Charlie. I should have forewarned you. It is a normal procedure to determine the strength of a man's neck muscles and the size of his neck. Those things are not always obvious. Nowadays I can guess at their height and weight and come close enough. If something does not look right, I will use a tape measure to take true measurements and weigh them with scales to be sure. But I do not often feel it is necessary, and I am not often wrong."

I sort of hoped Henker would hang around. He had aroused my curiosity and I would have liked to question him some. But he swigged some more whiskey and left right away, leaving me with my curiosity unsatisfied.

From his manner, I suspected he wasted as little time as possible in killing his man so as not to interfere with his drinking. He was more likely to do his talking in a saloon rather than idle chitchat with the likes of me. I supposed I would get a good look at his handiwork come morning and that would have to do.

No sooner had I sat down in the marshal's chair and propped my feet on his desk than the door opened again.

"Good evening, Charlie."

"Althea! What are you doing here?"

"I cannot remain sequestered in my quarters all the time, Charlie. Even I must be out and about with my errands from time to time. You must admit that I strive for discretion and attempt to avoid soiling the reputation of Los Santos with my presence in public, but still, I do have to show my face sometimes."

"That's not what I meant and you know it. What I meant was, why are you here, at the jail?"

"I wish to visit one of your prisoners. Harlow Mackelprang."

"Althea! What's got into you? I've heard you say more than once you wish you'd never see him again."

She didn't seem to have a ready answer for that one. It was almost as if she didn't know herself. As she thought it over, I allowed myself a good look at her.

Even though she was getting on in years for her line of work of professionally entertaining gentlemen callers—she had to be way up in her thirties—Althea was still a handsome woman and cut a striking figure. She was decked out in some pretty fancy duds. No plain housedresses for her. Her dress was a big, wide ruffled thing with lots of lace, sort of a pale purple in color. She wore a matching hat with a brim wider than a sombrero, and even carried a matching parasol all rolled up. Since the sun was already down, I figured it must be all for looks.

Studying her outfit made me think of what it covered. Like plenty of young men hereabouts, I had enjoyed Althea's favors—for a price, of course. Althea, as a matter of fact, introduced me to the earthly pleasures womankind offered. So I knew of the delights concealed beneath those few thin layers of fabric.

Then a picture of Becky wormed its way into my consciousness. I was a married man now, and I had best keep my thoughts where they belonged. Plenty of married men were among Althea's patrons, and I knew it. But I was determined not to be one of them. But as they say, time will tell. Time will tell.

"I can't say," Althea finally said. "I don't really know myself. It is something I feel compelled to do. Perhaps it will help me put bad memories to rest."

"Well, this is unusual. I'm not sure what Marshal would say. But I reckon it'll be all right. You want I should keep an eye on you while you're back there?"

"No, thank you, Charlie. I would appreciate privacy."

"There's another prisoner back there, you know."

"I suppose that will be as it must be."

"I'll be right here, Althea. If anything goes wrong, you just sing out and I'll be right there. I can't abide the thought of you coming to any more harm at the hand of Harlow Mackelprang than you already have."

She glided through the door in that classy way she has of moving, and I had to remind myself again to keep my mind at home where it belonged.

Within minutes, she stormed back into the office in an altogether different sort of locomotion and was out the front door in a flash. She didn't say a word and didn't even look my way. I barely had time to notice that her skin was flushed bright clean over her clenched jaw and on up over most of her face, and that she was breathing tight and fast through flared nostrils, almost like a snorty horse.

Figuring something unpleasant had happened, I beat it back into the lockup, fully intending to shoot Harlow Mackelprang dead if necessary.

It was immediately obvious that it would not be necessary. He was curled up on the floor of his cell whimpering and whining and clutching at his crotch. I guessed what Althea must have done to him, but did not bother to ask how or why she had done it. I figured he deserved it, whatever it was.

Once again I lowered myself into Marshal's chair hoping for a spell of uninterrupted relaxation. Not too much time passed, however, before the front door rattled opened again. This time I didn't have to wonder who it was or why they were there—it was the preacher, looking every bit the part in a black swallowtail coat and string tie over a white ruffle-front shirt. Come to think of it, there ain't much difference in the look of a Bible-thumper and cardsharp.

I sent him on through, wondering why he bothered showing up and thinking that whatever he did for Harlow Mackelprang, it wouldn't be as fitting as what the ruffian had gotten from Althea. The preacher was back there for quite a spell, and I could hear him raise his voice from time to time. Now and then the other prisoner, Sweeney, would pipe up too. I wondered if they were ganging up on Harlow Mackelprang, or what—but I didn't wonder about it enough to wander back and find out.

Instead, I shoved a few sticks of wood into the stove

and dumped some more water into the coffeepot along with a handful of grounds. I figured I'd need several cups of coffee to make it through until morning, so's I could attend the hanging with my eyes open. I wish it was some of that Arbuckle's from the café. We didn't even have any sugar here to take the edge off it. But it'll have to do.

So once it was warm enough, I splashed out a cupful and put my feet up, wishing for something to help pass the time.

I sure wish Becky was here.

Or maybe Althea.

MARIANO

Harlow Mackelprang's last supper just passed by.

Had I not been standing here by the door of the saloon watching the jailhouse down the way, I would not have known this thing. I would not have seen the deputy come out of the café, two doors down, carrying a tray covered with a cloth.

Had I not been standing just here just now, I would not have seen the gringo lawman stirring up dust and dodging horse manure as he angled across the street to the *cárcel*, passing through the door through which I myself passed yesterday.

Was it only yesterday? It seems so long ago. But at times like this, all time becomes one.

Yes. It *was* only yesterday.

"Whaddya want?" the marshal asked before I had even closed the door. I had caught him at his siesta, chair propped against the wall and stocking feet on the desk. I stood, head down, hat in hand, playing the lowly peon as he studied me through droopy eyelids.

Dropping his feet and the chair's legs to the floor, he rubbed his face roughly with the palms of his hands and said, "I know you. You're that greaser sumbitch runs with Harlow Mackelprang, ain't you."

"Oh, no, Señor. He is just a friend."

"Hmmph. That spindly reprobate ain't got no friends. I oughta lock you up on general principles. I bet I could round up some witnesses that would identify you as his accomplice in any number of criminal activities."

"*Qué?*" I asked, feigning confusion. I learned long ago that the easiest way to outsmart a know-it-all gringo is to act stupid.

"Oh, never mind, you ignorant greaser. Whaddya want?"

"I wish a word with *mi amigo, por favor.*"

"Planning a jailbreak, are you? Got the rest of the gang hiding out waiting for you and Harlow Mackelprang to hatch a plan?"

"*Qué?*"

"Aw, hell, never mind. Might as well talk to the wall. Got any weapons on you?"

"*Nada, señor.*"

"I can see you ain't got any that show. I'll search you anyway. I ain't never known a Mex that didn't have a blade tucked away somewheres."

He found nothing on me.

"Go on back. And no funny stuff, you hear?"

"*Sí, señor. Gracias, señor,*" I said, nodding and bowing like a coolie as I walked to the door that passed me through to the back of the building where the lock-ups were.

As with the marshal, I caught Harlow Mackelprang napping. He was lying on his back, stretched full length on the narrow cot. His hands were folded beneath his head for a pillow, elbows splayed, the heel of one boot resting atop the toe of the other. From all appearances, an unstable arrangement. But it must have suited him.

He was snoring loudly, and it struck me that in the three years I had known him, I had never seen Harlow Mackelprang so still. Normally he fidgeted and squirmed and paced, even tossing and turning in his sleep, as if his long skinny frame could not contain all the energy he generated.

I looked around the jail. There were three cells. Harlow Mackelprang was in the one closest to the door, so the marshal, I supposed, could keep an eye on him from the office. The center cell was empty. The one at the other end was occupied by a short fat man in a rumpled suit, complete with waistcoat and string tie.

"Hey, *gordo*, has he been sleeping long?" I asked.

He fished a pocket watch the size of a corn tortilla out of his vest and flipped open the lid. "Three hours and forty-two minutes this stretch, to be exact."

"Aye-yi-yi!"

"Sleeping like a baby! Sleeping the sleep of the innocent!" he said.

I could not help but laugh. "I am afraid you are very much mistaken, Señor."

"I do not often misjudge human nature. My livelihood depends on it."

I laughed again. "Judging from the size of the livelihood hanging over your belt buckle, that must be true. What keeps you so well fed?"

"Wealth. Security. Hope for the future."

"*Qué?*"

"Investments, sir. I deal in any number of financial instruments and opportunities. Insurance. Stocks.

Real estate. Mining. I also dabble in patent medicines and gilt-edged family Bibles with color plates."

"No wonder you are locked up instead of me. You are clearly the bigger crook."

"You insult me, sir. My reputation for honest dealing is well known throughout this territory and several states."

"What is your name, my friend, if you do not mind my asking?"

"Not at all, sir. Just call me Sweeney."

"So, Sweeney, if you are such an innocent of sterling reputation, what explains your presence in *cárcel de Los Santos?*"

"A simple misunderstanding, I assure you. One of the fine citizens of this community has accused me of fraudulently selling shares in a railroad incorporated in a distant state, but I assure you his investment is a fully legal and lawful transaction according to the printed terms of the contract. I have every confidence the courts will agree."

"So how come are you locked up? Why do you not post bond and stay at the hotel while waiting for your trial?"

"That is my wish, I assure you. But the complainant in my case happens to be one of the leading citizens of this burg. Vindictive bastard convinced the marshal to lock me up."

Again I laughed.

"Mariano, how come you got to make so much noise?"

The voice belonged to Harlow Mackelprang, but he had not stirred.

"Why do you sleep in the middle of the day, *jefe?*"

"Knock off that Mex talk. I've told you that a

million times. What the hell else am I supposed to do while I rot in this stinking jail in this stinking town waiting for you stinking idiots to bust me out of here? So what's the plan?"

"Is it wise to talk of such things with the marshal just there?" I whispered with a nod toward the office.

"Aw, hell, who cares. If we don't talk about it now, it'll be too late. In case you forgot, my hangin's day after tomorrow."

"Do not worry. I can assure you, we have not forgotten."

"Tell me one thing, Mariano. Where was you and that stupid McNulty when I came out of that bank?"

"It was the horses, *jefe*. Your horse got loose from McNulty and was getting away, and mine wanted to go away with him. You did not need me inside the bank, so I help my friend catch the horses. Then the marshal is coming, so we got out of there."

"So where's the rest of the fellers? They still around? Everybody here?"

By "everybody" he meant McNulty and Benito—the only two people on the face of the earth, besides me, still willing to ride with the infamous *bandido* and gunman Harlow Mackelprang. At one time we had been ten men, feared and respected on both sides of the border. Our coffers were always filled with coin; our saddlebags, with mescal; our stomachs, with food; and our *jacales*, with willing señoritas.

But that was before Harlow Mackelprang showed up that day half-starved and barely able to stay aboard the plow horse he rode. As it happened, Benito was standing guard the day the horse wandered through the gap. By abandoning his post to lead the half-dead man and sorry horse into camp, he aroused the ire of Catlin—Gato as I called him.

"Benito! What the hell you doin'? Who's watchin' the gap?" Catlin squalled like a furious feline.

Benito, of course, did not answer. Benito is mute and does not answer anyone. Not to my knowledge at least, and we are cousins and were boys in the same village and have been together all our lives. In all those years I have never heard a sound issue from his mouth, so I feel secure in saying none has ever done so, let alone the complex arrangements of sounds required to form words.

Besides being mute, Benito is slow in the head—not much, you understand, but enough that some will take advantage if allowed to do so. For this reason, I have always acted as something of a protector for *mi amigo*. So it was I who answered Gato.

"Do not worry about it. No one is looking for this place."

"Then how'd he get here?" Gato asked, indicating the then-unidentified Harlow Mackelprang.

He sagged in the saddle as if his bones had gone soft. A film of dust covered the man and his mount, thin enough in some places to allow their true colors to show through, but in such thick drifts in the wrinkles and hollows that the pair appeared to be an extension of the desert and could, for all practical purposes, have hidden in plain sight merely by staying still.

"Probably his horse smelled water. She looks like she needs a drink."

The only water to be found for miles—and miles—trickled out of the spring at the head of our hidden valley. I say "our" because it was used as a hideout by

those of us who rode with Gato. We often spent
time there after a job to allow things to cool down.
It had long been a hideout for thieves, at least since
the days when deserters from the conquering armies
of the Spanish became *bandidos* and plundered
colonies and rancheros with help from their Indian
accomplices.

The place did not appear on any maps of the
region—very little of anything appears on those
maps, as a matter of fact. Very few people frequented
those dry and desolate regions, so its very existence
was, for the most part, unknown. No one had even
bothered to give the place a proper name. We just
called it *el prado,* for a meadow it was.

As I said, the spring that watered *el prado* was the
only water for miles around. If one could fly with the
hawks (or the vultures), one would see this place as
a narrow green crescent surrounded by dirt and
rocks for as far as the eye could see in every direction; a green-bottomed crack in a brown hill, located
just a little farther from any other source of water
than most horses could travel before dropping dead.

The entrance was a narrow, twisted gap with sheer
rock walls. The trail dropped down slightly as one
rode through the gap, so the water from the spring
had no outlet. Had there been enough water to
form a lake, or even a pond, it would have turned
brackish, then salty, and *el prado* would have stran-
gled itself. But the spring produced only enough to
provide for the meadow, the few birds and animals
thereabouts, and the few humans and horses who
holed up there from time to time. Any surplus was
quickly swallowed up by the dry earth or evapo-
rated in the desert air.

Only a steep, narrow trail kept the place from being a box canyon—so while the gap provided the only true means of entering or leaving, if one knew where to find it, a skinny trail blazed by thirsty javelinas climbed the low cliffs near the spring.

El prado had always contributed to the mystery of the *bandidos* who hid out there. Pursuers told stories of the pursued simply disappearing into thin, hot air. Throughout history Spanish conquistadores, Mexican federales, U.S. cavalry detachments, and posses led by lawmen had suffered mightily and sometimes died for lack of water while attempting to find those who did not wish to be found and who knew how to find the hiding place of the meadow. Many times, manhunters who did find the place were massacred at the gap or allowed to enter *el prado* and then bottled up inside and wiped out.

But we did not wipe out Harlow Mackelprang. Perhaps it was because he seemed so helpless, barely alive and hardly able to stay mounted on his half-dead horse. Gato resigned himself to the man's presence and sent Benito back out on watch.

"Sophie!" Gato called. The redhead appeared in the door of a *jacal.* "Think you can keep this thing alive?"

She walked around the horse, looking the man up and down as if assessing his chances. "I reckon so. But why would I want to?"

"I admit he don't look like much," Gato said, "but he might prove to be of some use. Unless he's already on the wrong side of the law, I doubt he'd be out here."

It took a few days, but Sophie revived our visitor enough that he could once again speak. Restoring his voice was something we soon grew to regret.

We were told—at great length and with much repetition and, I suspect, much embellishment—of his misdeeds in the town of Los Santos and the killing of the farmer who had owned the horse he rode. He seemed pleased with himself for what he had done. It was as if he had discovered a new side of himself he had not known existed. His exploits, of course, paled in comparison to those of every member of Gato's band. But we did not attempt to disabuse Harlow Mackelprang's delusions of himself as a man worthy of our fear.

At the time, we did not believe he was worthy of our fear.

Only later would our opinions change.

Several weeks later, partly because of boredom with the quiet life in *el prado* and partly to test our guest's fitness for the outlaw life, Gato rode out to rob a stagecoach. He cared little which coach or what it carried—as I have said, his purpose this time lay elsewhere.

Our destination was the wagon road that led out of the mining district in the Thunder Mountains, in the belief that fortune might smile upon us and the stage would carry a mine payroll or other quantity of cash.

We rode out each leading two spare mounts. With two long days of hard riding ahead, we wanted fresh horses upon which to make our escape. Turning the used-up animals loose along the way back sometimes tended to confuse any posse that might be on our trail, particularly if they were local lawmen riding with reluctant volunteers.

By now, Harlow Mackelprang was well fed and rested, and only Benito escaped the consequences of his recovery. Lacking the ability to talk and showing no interest in listening, he was soon written off. The rest of us were not so fortunate.

Throughout the journey, Harlow Mackelprang rode first beside one of us, then another, assaulting each with questions about the life of the *bandido* and our experiences outside the law. Even more annoying, though, was his considerable boasting. There was no doubt in his mind that sneaking around Los Santos stealing inconsequential baubles and strutting about intimidating the weak and defenseless proved him *muy macho* and earned him a place among the hardened thieves and criminals in Gato's band. In his mind, shooting that unarmed farmer sealed the deal.

We granted him no such dispensation. A place among us would be earned or he would be cast aside like a pot of frijoles gone sour.

Upon reaching the appointed place for stopping stagecoaches on the Thunder Mountain road, Gato made assignments. Harlow Mackelprang was sent up the road to serve as lookout, with instructions to alert us upon the approach of the stagecoach. The rest of us retired to a concealed arroyo to wait, grateful for the quiet of his absence.

A few hours later, my siesta was interrupted by gunfire. Rifle fire—three or four shots at least. Even though the firing was somewhat distant, my guns were instinctively drawn. A minute or so later, another burst of gunfire, this time a pistol.

"*Qué pasa?*" I said.

Gato and the others looked equally puzzled.

"Damned if I know. We better go see what kind of trouble that mouthy kid is in," Gato said, so we tightened our cinches and rode into the hills to where we could circle back to the place from which Harlow Mackelprang was keeping watch. He was not there.

"Don't look like anything has happened here."

"Aah, but Gato, look. Something has happened down there. That little *cabrón* decided he did not need us."

Gato looked where I was pointing. A few hundred yards down the coach road, barely visible through a break in the cedar trees, we could see the overturned coach.

"Damn. Let's go take a look."

Harlow Mackelprang sat on a boulder beside the road, poking around in a broken strongbox and counting a stack of greenbacks. He ignored us until Gato reined up so close to where he sat that he could smell the horse's breath. After a few more seconds of make-believe counting, he looked up at Gato and flashed his stupid grin.

"Mr. Catlin, I believe there's enough here for us all," he said.

It was not difficult to reconstruct what had happened. From concealment just a few feet from the road, Harlow Mackelprang had gut-shot the shotgun guard, then put a couple of slugs into the off-wheel horse. Momentum rode the coach over the dead and dragging horse, capsizing it and upending the rest of the team. The pistol shots were apparently for the driver and to finish off the guard. He had not bothered with the horses. Besides the one he had shot to stop the coach, one was killed in the wreck. Another struggled to rise. The fourth horse was on its feet, but stumbling around on a broken leg.

I rode over to the crippled horse and put a bullet in its head.

"Madre de Dios, why do you not put these *caballos* out of their misery?" I asked, dismounting and shooting the broken animal still down and unable to get out of the tangle of harness and running gear.

"Aw, shit, Mariano. They're nothing but dumb animals. Why waste ammunition?" Harlow Mackelprang said.

I turned my pistol in his direction and pulled back the hammer. At the sound of the ratcheting metal, Harlow Mackelprang's eyes widened nearly to the size of silver pesos and his jaw hung loose below his likewise round mouth. I would have shot him had not Gato spoken.

"Put it away, Mariano. We best get out of here. This mess is sure to draw a lot more attention than I bargained for. Harlow Mackelprang, you stupid fool, I'll deal with you when I get the time."

The look of surprise already on Harlow Mackelprang's face spread, turned to hurt, and then to hate. The burning eyes seemed to smoke from the heat of things to come.

We stuffed our saddlebagsthe *dinero* from the box and rode away as the rear wheel of the stagecoach turned slowly in the wind. Events set in motion that day would take years to play out, but I sense the conclusion was already as determined as the rotation of that wheel on its hub.

Our only stop was at a remote watering hole to fill up our horses, canteens, and water skins. Harlow Mackelprang said little as we set off on a roundabout route back to *el prado*, but as the days passed and our destination neared, he boasted more and more of his feat.

"You shoulda seen the look on that shotgun rider's face," he said.

"That wheeler went down like a sack of shit," he said.

"Man, when that stage tipped over and crashed there was stuff a-flyin' ever-which-way," he said.

"I couldn't believe that guard weren't killed. I got him twice. Right in that big belly both times," he said.

"Well, he's sure 'nough dead now," he said.

"How much money you figger was in that box? Must be twelve, thirteen hunnerd dollars," he said.

"Looky here at this stubby shotgun. I reckon I'll be needin' it more from now on than that fat guard that used to carry it," he said.

"That driver mighta been dead when he hit the ground, but I didn't stop to ask. Shot him right in the head, is what I did," he said.

"Too bad there weren't any passengers. I coulda used the target practice," he said.

Laughing.

All the while laughing.

By the time we rode through the gap and into *el prado* he was in a fine humor and could not wait to share his heroism with those waiting there. But Gato cut his revelry short.

"I've heard more than enough about what an outlaw hero you are, Harlow Mackelprang, so you shut up. The truth is, you're stupid. That was a dumb thing to do and a dumb way to do it."

"We got the money, didn't we?"

"Yeah, we got the money. We also got two dead express company men. Which means we probably got a lot more people out looking for us than we need. Robbing a stagecoach don't attract near as much attention as murder, you idiot."

"You saying you ain't never killed nobody?"

"Hell, yes, I've killed people. But sometimes you can get what you want without killing no one, and most times that's the smart way to do it. I haven't lasted as long as I have at this outlaw business by shooting people just for the hell of it. And if you want to last with this outfit, Harlow Mackelprang, you'll do as I say and not pull any more stupid stunts. Otherwise you'll find out a thing or two about killing that you don't want to know." Gato did not wait for a reply, but turned on his heel and walked into his *jacal.*

"Catlin thinks he can push me around, he's got another think comin'," Harlow Mackelprang said to no one in particular.

"You mess with Gato, he will skin you alive," I told him.

"He messes with me, I'll kill him. I'll kill all you bastards if I have to," he said. "You better show me some respect or I'll show you."

Harlow Mackelprang did not kill all of us bastards. But he did kill some.

Gato rode out one day with most of us boys to hit a bank in Val Verde. Much to the boys' chagrin, Harlow Mackelprang was invited to stay behind.

When we returned to *el prado* two weeks later, it was to discover a fresh grave filled, we were told, with the remains of one of our *compadres*, a man named Hayslett. According to Harlow Mackelprang, Hayslett was cheating in a two-handed poker game. When called on it, he drew his gun and Harlow Mackelprang claimed he had no choice but to shoot. There being no witnesses, Gato accepted his word even though he did not believe him.

Simons, another of our number, soon rode away with the two señoritas, telling Gato he would come back and ride with him again when Harlow Mackelprang was gone—but that he would no longer expose the women to the insults and unwelcome advances of Harlow Mackelprang. Even a whore deserves respect, Simons said.

Keech left one night without explanation.

Sent out to help Dempsey and Larson knock off a stagecoach, Harlow Mackelprang came back alone except for the *dinero*. The story he told was that the shotgun guard had got them both before being killed himself.

But Gato learned a few days later that the guard died having never fired a shot, and that the posse found Dempsey and Larson shot dead out in the desert. So, instead of ten good men plus Harlow Mackelprang, our gang now numbered only six.

Gato confronted him about the dead-and-gone robbers.

"I'm down five men on account of you."

"You saying I killed Larson and Dempsey?"

"They weren't killed by the guard on the stagecoach. I know that. Maybe you better tell me what you know."

"I already told you."

"You're a liar, Harlow Mackelprang. I won't hold with no man who won't own up to what he does. You're nothing but a dangerous coward and I want you gone. You be out of here by morning. Take a spare horse. But be gone."

Gato walked away from the shade of the *ramada* where we sat.

Had he not embarrassed Harlow Mackelprang in our presence, things might have turned out differently. But I do not think so. The timing may have been different, but the result would have been the same, I think.

What happened is this: Harlow Mackelprang shot Gato in the back.

Gato hadn't walked ten paces before the angry and insulted Harlow Mackelprang scrambled to his feet, pulling and cocking his pistol as he rose. Gato must have heard or at least sensed the commotion. Why he did not react or respond I will never know. Nor will he. He underestimated Harlow Mackelprang— a thing he did not do concerning any other man in all the years I knew him.

It was a fatal mistake.

Harlow Mackelprang's first shot drilled a neat hole between our leader's shoulder blades. The bullet staggered him, but he did not fall. He started to turn, his benumbed right arm and hand waving uselessly near the butt of his holstered revolver, when a second shot shattered his knee, knocking his pins out from under him. Even as he fell, a third shot rang out, the lead whistling uselessly into the canyon wall as Gato's nose plowed a furrow in the dust.

Then the pistol turned on us, pointing alternately at me, Benito, McNulty, and Bucky.

"Any o' you bastards want to do anything about it?"

No one of us offered an answer.

"Good. I guess that puts me in charge of this outfit. I'll give the orders around here and you four will follow them. And I'm warning you right now—

you show me any disrespect and I'll shoot you on sight. Harlow Mackelprang ain't putting up with it no more. You all been hoorawin' and harassin' me ever since I been here. No more. Get it?"

Benito nodded.

The pistol pointed in turn to McNulty and Bucky, who also nodded. Then it was my turn.

"How 'bout you Mariano? You get it?"

"*Sí. Comprendo.* You will be the new *jefe*," I said, looking down the barrel.

"And that's another thing. Knock off that Mex talk. I don't never know what you're telling Benito when you jabber like that. Now on, we talk American around here."

I nodded my approval.

"Now scratch out a grave and bury Catlin. I don't want him stinkin' up this place no more. You got that?"

I nodded my assent.

By turns, with an old piece of drill steel and a rusty shovel stolen from one of the mining companies, we hacked out and hollowed a shallow grave at the edge of the growing *el prado* boneyard. As Bucky and McNulty finished off the final resting place of the famous outlaw who had unexpectedly become our former leader, Benito and I went to fetch the body.

We rolled his dead weight over onto his back so we could clean out his pockets and salvage anything of value from his person. Even in death, the surprise showed in Gato's wide-open eyes.

Bits of grit and grass speckled the surface of the eyeballs. My own eyes blinked without being asked, feeling, imagining, the stinging burn of that irritating foreign matter. Almost, I reached out to flick the bits away from his staring eyes, but did not.

Nor did I close the eyelids. Gato left this life wide-eyed and wondering, and it seemed to me fitting that he should greet the saints in heaven likewise.

Or, to say the truth of it, the devil in hell.

As Benito patted down the final shovelful of dirt on the mounded grave, our new *jefe* again graced us with his presence to assess the quality of our work.

"Sonofabitch looks about the same as always," he said. "Catlin wasn't worth dirt—and now he is dirt."

I had the feeling that Harlow Mackelprang had devoted all his thoughts since the shooting to the work of composing that phrase and practicing the timing of its delivery. He considered it amusing, laughing loud and long at his own cleverness.

"Now, you sorry bastards, take a good look at your big, bad outlaw leader. And never, never forget that you'll end up laying beside him if ever you cross Harlow Mackelprang."

To say we did not fear Harlow Mackelprang would be a lie. It would be foolish not to fear such a man. I have known many bad men in my life. But this one, this one was more than just bad—he was *muy loco*. He found insane pleasure in forcing others to his will, whether it was his will for them to be robbed or raped, to bawl and beg, to live or die.

And he had something that even many of the worst of the bad men lacked: the willingness to kill without thought or hesitation.

So why would we stay with such a man for more than two years to come? When I say "we," I speak of McNulty, Benito, and myself. Bucky decided that something better was in store for him, and rode out to the gap for sentry duty one night and kept riding.

Why did the rest of us not ride away as well?

I think it was because he feared us as much as we feared him. As I had nearly killed him once before, he knew I would do so should the need arise. He had always been uncomfortable around Benito—one who talked as much as Harlow Mackelprang could not fathom so much quiet in another. That, and the fact that I looked after the simple-minded Benito, prevented him from taking advantage.

McNulty was no longer young and cared little about living or dying. Nor did he care to seek out another band to throw in with. His ambivalence concerning his fate, combined with his ability as a *pistolero*, kept Harlow Mackelprang at bay—for while both had the will to kill, McNulty had the greater skill.

Thus we hung together in an uncomfortable kind of equilibrium. From time to time we would withdraw funds from a train or a bank or a stagecoach, ranging widely across the region.

While Gato had protected his anonymity as much as possible, Harlow Mackelprang desired notoriety. And he achieved it through many rash acts of unnecessary killing and cruelty. A collection of wanted posters resided in his saddlebags, and he would often look them over with glee, impressed with his fame as a *bandido* and murdering gunman.

This hunger for the limelight allowed the rest of us to remain nameless and faceless for the most part, simply accomplices of Harlow Mackelprang, lurking in the shadows.

We three spent a good deal of time at *el prado*, but our *jefe* was too high-strung for such solitude. He traveled far and wide by himself, sometimes boasting and bullying in cantinas and sometimes sneaking around. He bragged to us often of secretive visits to a "lady friend" in his hometown of Los Santos. And he always showed us the most recent additions to his collection of Harlow Mackelprang reward dodgers.

His ability to elude capture was impressive. He learned many tricks and invented some of his own. But when he was finally tracked to *el prado,* making it necessary for Benito to dispatch a determined bounty hunter as he entered the gap, it became clear that Harlow Mackelprang had become too much of a liability.

There would be no satisfaction in simply killing Harlow Mackelprang. So we devised a plan utilizing his own vanity as a weapon against him.

"So, *jefe,* have you visited Los Santos of late?"

"Stop calling me that, Mariano. It's been a while since I was there. Why?"

"Oh, nothing, Señor. Just curious. What do the people of your hometown say about Harlow Mackelprang, the bad hombre?"

"Damned if I know. I don't see no one there except for Althea."

"Aah, *sí.* Your ladyfriend, no?"

"Yep. That she is."

"So is she pleased to see you?"

"Damned if I know. Don't much care neither. She sees me whether she wants to or not. Makes no never mind to me if she's happy about it. I slip into town, visit Althea, and I'm gone before anyone else even knows I been there."

"Why is that, *jefe?* Does the notorious *bandido* fear capture by the law?"

"Shit!" Harlow Mackelprang said. "Marshal there is so dumb he couldn't catch his own ass with both hands. He ain't nothin' but an old soldier with a gimpy leg."

"So you do not respect him then."

"Hell, no."

"But does he respect you?"

This gave Harlow Mackelprang cause for consideration, so I left him alone with his thoughts for a time. Another day, our talk of Los Santos continued.

"We have never visited Los Santos, Señor. Could we not go there and relieve your former neighbors of some of their money?"

"Ain't much there. One little bank. Express office at the train station."

"We do not need the money. We will do it for the enjoyment. And surely the people of Los Santos would enjoy being robbed by Harlow Mackelprang, the famous *bandido* from their hometown."

"Tell you the truth, Mariano, I wouldn't mind sticking my pistol up a few noses in that town. Teach them peckerwoods some respect."

"Perhaps. Perhaps. Ah, but we will probably be captured. The law will be alerted as soon as you are recognized."

"I ain't worried about that. We could be in and out before that gimpy old marshal could limp across the street."

"I don't know, *jefe*. . . ."

"I do, Mariano. We're doin' it. We'll rob the bank. Why the hell not? That bank horn-swoggled me one time and it's about time I settled the account. I'll make that banker and all them other hoity-toity folks in Los Santos wish they'd never messed with Harlow Mackelprang."

His plan was a simple one.

Benito would wait outside of town with the spare horses.

Harlow Mackelprang, McNulty, and I would ride into town.

In the street in front of the bank, Harlow Mackelprang and I would dismount.

McNulty would lead our horses away, staying nearby but away from the bank to avoid attention.

Harlow Mackelprang would lead the way into the bank with his sawed-off shotgun and collect the money.

I would wait inside the door, covering the people in the bank who were not occupied with Harlow Mackelprang.

A simple plan, as I say, that had worked many times.

But it was not the plan Benito, McNulty, and I followed.

This is our plan, and this is what happened.

When we dismounted in front of the bank, McNulty dropped the reins to ground-tie my horse, then rode down the dusty street to the marshal's office, where he reported a bank robbery in progress. Once Harlow Mackelprang was about his business inside the bank, I slipped out, mounted up, and rode with McNulty out of town to where Benito awaited, then off into the desert.

A simple plan, but an effective one. This is the way, I am told, the rest of it happened.

"C'mon, hurry it up!" Harlow Mackelprang shouted at the frightened clerk. "Get the money in the sack or I'll blow your damn head off!"

Behind the clerk, the vice president of the bank stood beside his desk with his hands raised, as instructed. He was a short and skinny man with a bald head with a wispy blond fringe. His neatly trimmed mustache was a darker shade of blond, his suit a shade darker still. He wore a watch chain, a pocket hanky, and a pair of gold-rimmed spectacles. His name was Tueller.

"C'mon, dammit! Ain't you done yet? Hurry it up!"

"You won't get away with this, you know," the clerk stammered as he stuffed coin and currency from the cash drawers into the bag.

"Shut up. Get finished."

"That's it. That's all there is."

"Now empty that safe."

The safe was a small one, sitting on the floor behind where Tueller stood.

"There isn't much here," the clerk said as he transferred the few stacks of bills and some gold coins into the bag. "You won't get away with this."

"Bring it! And shut up.

"Mariano! We clear? McNulty there?

"Give me that sack!

"Mariano!?"

Harlow Mackelprang cast a quick glance toward the door. I cannot even imagine what thoughts occurred to him when he realized that I was gone and he was alone.

"Shit! Mariano! Where you at?" he said as he backed slowly toward the door.

The clerk said, "You won't get away with this. We know who you are."

"Shut up!"

"You're Harlow Mackelprang."

"Damn right I am! And don't you forget it!" he screamed as the sawed-off shotgun boomed.

Tueller winced as bits of gore from the clerk splattered his tan suit, speckled his eyeglasses, and stuck to his face. But he did not move.

As the robber ran through the open door, the one good leg the marshal possessed lashed out from where the lawman was pressed against the wall, tripping up Harlow Mackelprang, sending the stubby shotgun and money sack tumbling, and leaving the bandit sprawled facedown on the boardwalk.

He gathered his wits and started to rise, but was forced back down by the barrel of a gun pushed into the back of his head.

"You even try to get up and I'll blow you to hell, Harlow Mackelprang," the Marshal said.

Our *jefe* languished in jail for two weeks awaiting the arrival of the circuit judge to conduct the trial, which lasted less than an hour.

"Harlow Mackelprang, you are a cold-blooded killer who has terrorized this territory for too long. But you have beaten and burned and robbed and stolen and murdered your last. The jury having returned a verdict of guilty in this case, I cheerfully sentence you to die, die, die. One week hence you will be hanged by the neck until you are dead. Perhaps the Good Lord will be more kindly disposed to show you mercy than this court is—but I hope not. May you burn in hell for the duration of eternity!" the judge said, and slammed down his gavel.

Following the bank robbery, Benito, McNulty, and I had waited in the desert, slipping into Los Santos from time to time for news of Harlow Mackelprang. We learned the details of his arrest. We were told of his trial. We knew the day he would die.

And so it was that yesterday I visited him at the jail, not wanting Harlow Mackelprang's last days on earth to be without hope.

"So, what's the plan?" he asked.

"Do not worry. All things happen in time."

"You coming tonight?"

"I do not think tonight. *Mañana.*"

"Tomorrow then. In daylight? You think that's a good idea?"

"Aah, *jefe,* I think you are right—it is not a good idea. We will not come tomorrow."

"Damn. Just like two dumb Mexicans and an old man to leave things until the last minute. Where are the others anyway?"

"Do not worry. They wait outside of town. You will not see them in Los Santos until the appointed time."

"Well, you damn sure better get it right. You mess up and it's my neck."

"*Sí, señor,* I know that. And now I will go."

I have not returned to visit again. I have given him all the hope I can. Now, I can only hope that he will enjoy the supper that just passed by this place, on a tray covered with cloth.

In the morning he will hang. And when he has climbed the gallows, and after the noose is around his neck, and before the bag is placed over his head, I hope he looks out over the people assembled there. I hope he sees Mariano, Benito, and McNulty sitting quietly on our horses at the far edge of the crowd.

And I hope the last thing Harlow Mackelprang realizes in this life is that those two stupid Mexicans and that old man waited too long to save him.

MARSHAL

Harlow Mackelprang's last supper was just slid under the bars into his cell, and sits there on the floor waiting to be devoured.

And I do mean devoured. I have been amazed these past three weeks how much food that skinny ingrate puts away and how fast he shovels it in. At least that's the case for the usual plain fare of beans and biscuits we feed prisoners. We'll see if it goes for the steak dinner he requested as his final meal.

I hope he chokes on it.

On second thought, I hope he don't. I do not want to deprive the people of Los Santos the enjoyment of seeing Harlow Mackelprang swing. This town hasn't had a minute's peace since he came here as a five-year-old boy. Even these past three years when he was hiding out in the desert running with that gang of thieves and killers, I slept with one eye open, expecting his return.

Sad to say, my expectations were more than met.

We lost track of the little thug the day after he tore up the town and shot Soren out at his farm. Maybe if I hadn't been so surprised by him slapping Althea around and shooting up the saloon, I could have got a posse up sooner and stopped Harlow Mackelprang before he shot Soren and stole his horse and goods.

We did have the fire at the stable to put out, true, but I've always been bothered that maybe I could have saved a lot of pain had I acted faster. Not only the pain Soren's death has caused Lila and their kids, but all the other grief he has spread through these parts since he left here, and the murder he did here when he finally came back.

At least it will all be over come morning.

"He's fed, Marshal," Charlie, my deputy, said as he passed out of the lockup and through the office door.

"For the last time, I hope."

"Me too. Packing grub for them lowlifes we keep locked up back there is my most unfavorite part of this job."

"Yeah, I know," I said. "But don't forget that if it wasn't for them lowlifes that break the law, there wouldn't be no lawman job. For you or anybody else."

"I reckon you're right. Even still, it's all I can do sometimes to keep from taking a leak in their coffee."

"Go on home, Charlie, and get you some supper. Then come on back and keep an eye on things, so I can get some shut-eye. I don't want to be dozy come the morning's festivities."

"See you in a while then," he said as he passed through the jailhouse door to make his way home to a hot supper with his pretty new wife, Rebecca. Becky, she goes by. She don't cotton much to Charlie's occasional night duty. Give her a few years and she won't mind nearly so much. Lucky for her, night duty at the jail isn't necessary all that often—only when a badder-than-average desperado like Harlow Mackelprang is locked up.

But I don't expect any difficulty, so Charlie should be fine. I've been keeping my eye on that Mexican that came by to visit yesterday, but all he's done is hang around the saloon with another Mex and an old man. Them three fit the descriptions on some of these reward dodgers in my desk. I swear they're Harlow Mackelprang's lackeys. But they don't act like they got anything planned.

And funny thing, I'd lay odds that that old man was the one who tipped us off about the bank robbery that led to Harlow Mackelprang's capture. But I couldn't swear to it.

That had to have been one of the strangest crimes gone wrong in all of history. I certainly never heard of nothing like it.

Charlie and I were just lazing around the office that quiet afternoon, me with my feet on the desk to give my game leg a rest and Charlie on the only other chair in the place, propped against the wall by the door. Someone outside the door called out—not loud nor excited, but insistent.

"Marshal! Step out here a minute, will you."

Being closer to the door, not to mention younger and quicker, Charlie was on his feet before I had even got around to reacting. He cast me a questioning glance, so I nodded for him to go on. He opened the door and poked his head out.

"Yeah, what is it?"

"Harlow Mackelprang's robbing the bank. You

might want to get on over there. But be on your toes. I seen a scattergun."

"What?" I heard Charlie say as I made my way to the door. I hoped to ask that question myself, but the man was already riding off. I didn't get much of a look at him, but he looked like his best years were behind him. He rode down the street in the direction of the bank, leading a saddle horse. Just in front of the bank another man—dark-skinned fellow, looked Mexican—was getting mounted. Then the two spurred up their horses and headed out of town at a long trot, leading that third horse.

Saying all that, it may sound like me and Charlie was standing there with our faces hanging out watching the whole thing. But no. We were quickstepping it down the sidewalk toward the bank.

"He say it was being robbed *now?*" I asked.

"That's what it sounded like to me."

"I thought so too. We best not take any chances. You make yourself small in the alley there next to the bank. I'll get up next to the door, see if I can figure out what's up."

"Right," Charlie said, sounding about half-nervous and all the way afraid, which seemed appropriate in the circumstances. We were crossing the alley just then.

"Get that pistol in your hand where it'll do some good," I whispered as I stepped up onto the sidewalk in front of the bank. I could hear Harlow Mackelprang sounding all agitated and yelling something about "Mariano," and I could hear Calvin, the bank clerk, telling him something to the effect that he knew who he was and he wasn't going to get away with it, and the robber yelling something back at him.

About then the shotgun went off.

I was just beside the door when I heard the clomp of footsteps coming my way. The door banged open and them feet kept coming, so without even thinking about it, I stuck the foot on the end of my good leg out there to send them feet and whoever was attached to them tumbling.

It worked. Harlow Mackelprang went sprawling facedown all over that sidewalk, his gangly arms and legs going all directions, dropping a sack and a sawed-off shotgun in the process.

In a step and a half I was beside his head, just as he commenced to raise up. I stopped him by boring the barrel of my pistol into the back of his neck.

"You even try to get up and I'll blow you to hell, Harlow Mackelprang," I said.

He didn't, so I didn't.

"Charlie!" I called, and he stepped around the corner. "Get some handcuffs on him." Once the cuffs were in place, I had Charlie hobble Harlow Mackelprang with a short piece of rope.

"You just lay right there. I'll deal with you in a minute," I said to Harlow Mackelprang. "If he moves, shoot him," I told Charlie. "I better see what kind of mess he made in there."

Dreading what I'd find, I entered the bank. I found about what I feared. First thing I saw was Tueller, standing there looking like someone dumped a bucket of slaughterhouse guts all over him. There was blood dripping off his face and bits of meat plastered all over him. Blood covered most of his suit. Even his eyeglasses and bald head were spattered. I thought he'd been shot, but realized all the blood was on his outside and didn't come out of him.

I stood there looking at Tueller, and he stood there with his hands raised staring like he was fixed on something in the far, far distance. On the floor between us was the bank clerk, Calvin. At least what of him wasn't splattered all over Tueller and painting the surrounding area a hundred shades of red.

"You all right, Tueller?" I asked quietly. He didn't answer. Just kept staring at nothing. "Tueller?" Finally, I stepped around the mess on the floor and took hold of his arm and gave it a little shake. "Tueller—c'mon, snap out of it."

He turned, ever so slow, and looked at me. Slowly, his eyes sort of came into focus and he became aware of my presence.

"Marshal. Oh, my God, Marshal," he said slowly. "It was Harlow Mackelprang. He killed Calvin."

"I know it. We've arrested him. You can put your hands down now. It's all over."

Slowly, still dazed, he dropped his hands. I about told him not to worry, that everything was fine. But I realized how stupid and wrong that would sound.

"C'mon," I said instead, "let's get you home so you can get cleaned up. We'll get Calvin taken care of and I'll find someone to mop up in here."

The place was a hell of a mess. From the look of things, Harlow Mackelprang had been only a few steps away from Calvin when he cut loose with that sawed-off shotgun. And Calvin had been only a few steps from Tueller.

Had the shot been fired from any more distance, Tueller likely would have caught some buckshot himself in the scatter. But as it was, Calvin caught the full load right in the middle and it had pretty much cut him in half. So all Tueller got hit with was a good portion of what used to be Calvin.

I sent Charlie to escort Tueller to his house, and told him to then go around and fetch the undertaker to gather up what was left of the bank clerk and have him see the mess got cleaned up. The floor, the wall, and Tueller's desk would all require a quantity of soap and water and elbow grease.

Then I hustled Harlow Mackelprang down the street to the jailhouse. Since Tueller wasn't in any condition to deal with it, I scooped up the money sack along with the empty shotgun and took them along with me.

I shoved Harlow Mackelprang into the cell closest the door, and smacked him a good one on the back of the head with the butt-end of that shotgun, not wanting to take any chances in getting off those hobbles and handcuffs, then slammed the door shut and locked it. I tossed that sack of money onto the cot in the empty cell and locked that door too, thinking it would be safe there and its presence might remind the prisoner just how stupid he was.

Figuring I'd earned it, I walked over to the saloon for a whiskey to calm my nerves. I didn't take advantage of it often, but the barkeep there was always willing to stand me to drinks. Sort of a reward for public service, if you know what I mean.

After pouring back a few and telling the latest crime news to the layabouts who frequented the saloon, I wandered back over to the jail. By that time, our prisoner was awake and sitting on the cot, elbows on knees and head in hands.

He was so damn long and skinny, he looked like

a jumble of tree twigs bound with binder twine. Sort of made you wonder how all those gangly appendages didn't get tangled up among themselves when he walked. Watching him gather it all up and run was truly a sight to behold. Thinking of it almost brought a smile to my face, but seeing him sitting there in the cell, I just shook my head sadly instead.

"Harlow Mackelprang, what the hell were you thinking, shooting that young man like you did?" I asked him through the bars. "There weren't enough money in that bank to be worth killing for."

"That fool kept up saying I wouldn't get away with it. That I'd get caught. That they knowed who I was and they'd get me. Well, I guess I showed him ain't no one tells Harlow Mackelprang what he will and won't do."

"But as it turns out, he was right. You didn't get away with it."

"Well, that sissy office boy with his soft hands and starched collar might have been right, but he's dead all the same. So I guess he learned his lesson, didn't he."

I had no reply for that. Someone as thickheaded as Harlow Mackelprang ain't likely to understand just how silly that kind of thinking is. One thing I've noticed in my years dealing with criminals is that more often than not they're as dumb as a dull ax. And what's worse, they're too dumb to even know they're dumb.

Most folks come to realize their limitations after life stomps 'em down a time or two. Then they either learn from their shortcomings or figure out how to compensate for them or both. But your average outlaw, as I said, is plumb stupid, so I couldn't see much sense in trying to talk sense to Harlow Mackelprang.

So I changed the subject.

"Haven't seen you around town for quite a spell. Can't say I've missed you."

"But you did miss me, Marshal. I been back to Los Santos lots of times."

"Yeah, I know that. Althea's told me about your little visits." Althea is the local lady of the evening, only she ain't no lady and she ain't particular about the time of day should someone show up with cash in hand.

According to her, all Harlow Mackelprang ever showed up with, on those dark mornings he'd steal into town and come tapping on her door, was a mean streak a mile wide. I saw the result of his visits on Althea's face plenty of times—fat lips, black eyes, bruised cheeks, a bent nose. It was enough to make Althea complain that the cash she slipped me in those perfumed envelopes every month to keep her out of trouble wasn't buying her much protection.

But that's another story.

"What I mean is," I said to Harlow Mackelprang, "you've kept yourself pretty scarce. Most folks thought they were rid of you for good."

"Shows what they know."

"Myself, I always figured you'd be back. Fact is, I didn't think it'd take this long for you to miss the folks back home."

"Well, I been kinda busy."

"I know that. I been keeping up with your doin's. Got a pretty good stack of posters on you," I said.

"How about that, Marshal!" he said. "I been collectin' them things myself. I specially like the ones with the pictures on them. Pretty good likeness, don't you think?"

"Not bad. Not nearly ugly enough, though. Course, maybe that's on account of I know you too well. I can't look at you without seeing your meanness show through."

That meanness sure showed in his crimes. As I said, I had kept up with his comings and goings as best I could. And here's what Harlow Mackelprang got up to after giving us the slip after he set fire to the stable and shot Soren, as near as I can figure it out.

Within a month or two, there was a stagecoach robbery over around the Thunder Mountains. The reports said the stage was crashed and the shotgun guard and driver both killed. It took a while, of course, for the stage to be missed and located, and by the time the law arrived the trail had gone cold.

The getaway had all the marks of the Catlin gang, what with used-up horses scared off on false trails to confuse trackers, trails branching off as the gang split up, and a general direction leading toward the middle of the driest and most desolate part of hell. There have always been stories of a hideout and water out there somewhere, but no one has ever found it that I know of. And I know of some who died looking.

But as I said, while the getaway looked like Catlin, the crime didn't. As a matter of fact, I heard through the grapevine that Catlin himself sent word to the sheriff over there in Trueno that he had nothing to do with the killing. Within a year or so, they say Catlin dropped off the face of the earth and his gang pretty much broke up.

No one ever said so as far as I know, but I suspect

Harlow Mackelprang had a hand in Catlin's disappearance and the breakup, as he picked up some of the pieces of the old gang and formed a bunch that was worse than Catlin's outfit ever was. Whereas Catlin tended to avoid violence, once Harlow Mackelprang got involved—starting with that Thunder Mountain stage robbery, if you ask me—pistol-whipping and shooting and killing were more important than stealing money or cattle or horses or whatever. Terror was their real stock in trade, and Harlow Mackelprang never missed a chance to make it known that he was the man to be feared.

Take that time they rustled a band of sheep down near the border. While a couple of outlaws gathered up them brush maggots and drove them away, Harlow Mackelprang shot the Mexican herder in both his feet, then tied him to his horse. That herder said the *bandido* told him to thank his boss for such a fine band of sheep, and to say that "Harlow Mackelprang wants more just like them." Then he spooked the herder's horse into a runaway.

Lucky for that Mex, the horse eventually made its way back to the home ranch. That way, he was able to deliver that message and spend the rest of his life hobbling and crawling around, a cripple, rather than dying in the desert.

Harlow Mackelprang rustled a mixed herd of cattle one time, shooting up and killing most of the crew of cowboys and vaqueros who had just rounded them up. But trailing herds of livestock down into Mexico deep enough to find a buyer takes time and effort, and Harlow Mackelprang never cottoned much to a job of work, so rustling soon enough dropped off his list of ways to make a living.

Then there was the time the gangly fool and his band robbed a passenger train. A passenger train! They didn't even open up the mail car, where there might have been a money shipment or a safe with something in it worth taking. Hell, no! What they did was, while two or three men held the engine crew and conductor at gunpoint, Harlow Mackelprang paraded through both passenger coaches pretending to be a fearsome gunman and relieving folks of pocket money. And he shot a man in each car—one of them died—just to get folks' attention.

"Now you know Harlow Mackelprang means business," he told them.

I tell you, I always knew that kid was stupid and mean. But once he decided to become a notorious bandit, he surprised even me with his extremes on both counts.

He once robbed the bank over in Robbinsville, but wasn't satisfied with the take, so he knocked two customers and a clerk over the head and tied them up and set the place on fire. The building burned to the ground, but passersby was able to drag those folks out in time.

He robbed another stagecoach on the Thunder Mountain run, repeating his mean trick of hiding in the brush and shooting a wheel horse. This time, though, the driver managed to stop the team before the Concord coach overturned.

In the confusion of calming the horses and keeping them from bolting like they were inclined to do, what with them being hitched together with one of their kind bleeding and dying, Harlow Mackelprang climbed up over the boot and shot the driver in the back of the head, then gunned down the guard, who fell among the hooves and further upset the horses. As they bolted, the bandit barely managed to throw down the strongbox and jump overboard before being carried away on the runaway stage.

The frightened team ran on down the road some three miles before they were spent. All the way, they dragged along the dying, then dead near-side wheeler, and what life may have been left in the shotgun guard was rubbed out in the ruts and potholes in the rough wagon road.

The passengers in the coach, a mine officer's wife and daughter setting out on a visit to her folks in Ohio, were so frightened by the whole affair that she sent word to her husband that they may never come back. She claims the remembered sound of Harlow Mackelprang's boot steps overhead on that coach roof still wakes her up screaming in the middle of the night.

The worst thing was, I got a report about six months ago about Harlow Mackelprang getting drunk and disorderly up north a ways in Madera. That place ain't really a town, just a roadhouse, so there's no formal law there. I guess that's why he wasn't afraid of being arrested while hanging around for days at a time.

Anyway, word was he got surlier than usual when he got stewed one day and was annoying folks, so the bartender—a man name of Murphy, whose place it was—smacked him on the head with a sap and locked him in a shed out back to sober him up. After a good deal of hollering and pounding, he was let loose the next day, given his guns, and told not to come back.

But he did come back. He waited until the middle

of the night when everything was quiet, and he sneaked into that man's bedroom and hit him over the head with a stove poker. When Murphy woke up he was in the saloon, bound hand and foot and roped to a chair. Once he got his bearings, Murphy saw that his wife and their only overnight guest were also tied to chairs.

The details of what happened next aren't fit for human consumption so I won't go into them much. Suffice it to say that Harlow Mackelprang shot the lodger in the back of the head.

"Just so you and the lady know I mean business," he said to Murphy.

Then he ripped the nightclothes off the woman, and Murphy had to watch while unspeakably filthy things were done to his wife. Finally, Harlow Mackelprang gut-shot Murphy twice so the woman could watch him bleed out and die.

"I guess that'll teach him not to mess around with Harlow Mackelprang," he told the woman before leaving her there to be found by freighters who happened by the next day.

Like I said, I have known Harlow Mackelprang about as long and as well as anyone, and I never guessed he would come to such a bad end or cause so much trouble along the way. Oh, I knew—everybody in town knew—that he would come to no good. But I didn't imagine I'd be seeing his name on so many wanted posters for so many killings.

Nor did I imagine I would be the one to escort him to the gallows and stand by while the hangman pulls the lever that will drop him through the door to hell.

Matter of fact, I did not even imagine that I would have to put up with people like Harlow Mackelprang when I took this lawman job. For that matter, I never even planned to be a lawman.

My life was in the Army, where I spent a dozen years as a private soldier following the routine path of postings and promotions, waiting for a chance to distinguish myself. Which finally happened when I was just shy of thirty years old—but not in the way I hoped.

It was while my cavalry outfit was assigned to Fort Tecumseh up in Indian Territory, and what happened was one of those silly accidents that defy explanation. We were saddling up for patrol and I was pulling the slack out my cinch when a dogfight broke out.

Them useless curs were everywhere at once, including among and around our tethered mounts. There were three of them in the fight, but they made as much racket as three times that many. Their rolling and spinning and growling and yowling spooked more than a few horses, including mine, and he managed to knock me over with his hindquarters with all his hopping around. While I was down, another horse (felt more like a whole herd of them) stomped me up one side and down the other.

After spending a number of weeks in the infirmary healing from my "wounds," I walked out with a limp from a mashed-up knee that's stiff to this day. Oh, it has some bend to it, enough to sit a saddle. But it could not then, nor can it yet, stand up to the long hours of horseback that cavalry duty requires. Nor did my gimpy leg equip me for service as a dragoon or a foot soldier. Which left a desk job, for which I had neither the rank, the qualification, nor the inclination.

So I quit the service of my country, and through

circumstance and happenstance found myself in Los Santos with a badge pinned to my shirt.

When it comes to towns, Los Santos ain't nothing special. If not for a more-or-less-permanent supply of water from springs that form the headwaters of a creek (although we call it a river), it probably wouldn't be here at all. But when they laid rails through this country over to one of the mining districts, this was one of the few places to take on water and the town is the result.

Having a source for supplies made it easier for the stock-raising outfits hereabouts, and there's even farms along the creek bottom for miles downstream until the river peters out and the desert soaks it up.

All in all, a law-abiding place. Oh, now and then I would have to lock up a cowhand from one of the outlying ranches for blowing off too much steam, and miners passing through sometimes got too rough.

But most of the traffic through here was salesmen and business types on the way to and from the mines over in the mountains. So for the most part it was a pretty quiet life for the law in Los Santos. As much as anything, we were here for appearances.

I won't pretend that all that changed when Harlow Mackelprang came to town. Hell, he was just a five-year-old kid at the time. But the seeds were planted, and it wasn't long before the little brat became an irritant—you know, like a pebble in your boot.

He showed up here with his dad nineteen, twenty years ago. He didn't have no ma. Apparently, she had took sick and died up in the mining towns a few years before, when Harlow Mackelprang weren't but a toddler. His dad had took it hard and took up drinking.

Though he swears it ain't so, drunkenness probably

played a part in the mining accident that hurt his back and left him unfit for any kind of hard work. His hard drinking wasn't affected. So about the only work he ever does is cleaning up after folks—swabbing out the saloon, keeping the café and the hotel clean, mucking stalls at the stable, mopping up here at the jail, and suchlike.

But he never lets working interfere with his real job, that of being an alcoholist.

As you could guess, he did not devote much time to the proper raising of his boy. Harlow Mackelprang wandered the streets and fended for himself best he could.

He would beg a little something to eat out behind the café from time to time, or at some kind woman's back door. He hadn't the sense to be grateful about it, though, so that kind of kindness tapered off and he replaced it by thieving food.

Kitchen gardens were fair game, and he'd steal eggs right out from underneath a hen. Milk from the cooling house, spuds from a root cellar, meat from a smokehouse—it all tasted good to Harlow Mackelprang and he wouldn't hesitate to help himself.

From stealing food, the boy graduated to stealing anything that wasn't nailed down. Some of it so strange and useless to him that he must have stole it purely out of meanness.

Why, he once stole a small keg of nails from the mercantile! That mystery wasn't solved until nearly a year later when someone happened upon the busted keg in a dry wash outside town. The nails were scattered from hell to breakfast, just laying out there in the dirt turning to rust—as much as anything can rust in this country.

But the strangest thing he ever took was old Detmer's fiddle. Any time that old man tucked that instrument under his chin you could count on a good time. So folks was right put out when that fiddle was found, the morning after a schoolhouse dance, smashed to bits and stuffed into a rain barrel down by the train station.

Of course no one saw Harlow Mackelprang take it. No one hardly ever saw him take anything. But you just knew it was that kid, if you know what I mean.

It wasn't just thieving either. He'd bust up things too. I can't even tally how many windows he smashed. Once he got into the schoolhouse at night (one of the few times he ever set foot in the place after being tipped over in the outhouse), and upset desks and book presses, scattered papers, spilled inkwells, and ripped up books.

I said he didn't go to school much, but that don't mean he wasn't around there. He'd steal lunches from anyone littler than him and start fights and pester kids at recess. He even took to "borrowing" the out-of-town kids' horses during class and he'd use them hard, racing around out in the desert.

When it came to being mean to animals, it wasn't just horses with Harlow Mackelprang. He would torment dogs about any time he'd find one tied up, so it couldn't get at him. No one could ever prove it, but everyone knew it was him who would sneak around after dark and pour coal oil on barn cats, then light them afire. Every now and then a sheep or a cow would turn up dead, sometimes all cut up and mutilated right in someone's backyard, or cowhands would come across cattle that had been shot for no reason other than target practice, it seemed.

Quite often, folks would hear something outside their houses at night or think they'd see a face at a window, but by the time they got out the door, there was nothing to find but the sound of footsteps running off in the dark.

Althea only caught him at it twice, but she complained regularly that Harlow Mackelprang was all the time peeking in at her whilst she was entertaining guests. Not that Althea was modest, understand—but her guests liked their privacy and she feared his skulking around was bad for business. I can only imagine what kind of an education a growing boy might get peering through those windows.

Well, I could go on and on about Harlow Mackelprang's adventures as a budding criminal. I suppose I already have. Now here I sit watching him shovel down the last supper he'll eat in this world.

I wonder how he'll behave in the morning. It's possible, I suppose, he could face it like a man. More likely, he'll snivel and whine like the low-down coward he is. I'm about halfway sorry I don't get to hang him myself. Then again, it'll be nice to just sit back and relax and watch this professional neck-stretcher the judge sent for do the deed without me having to worry about it.

When Charlie gets back, I think I'll mosey over to the café and fill my own gullet. That's one good thing about being the law in this town. When it comes to paying for meals at the café, I don't offer and they don't ask. After that, I think I could maybe use another drink.

Morning can't get here soon enough.

McNULTY

Harlow Mackelprang's last supper will sit a lot easier on his stomach if mixed with a little whiskey.

Mariano just saw the deputy taking a meal tray over to the jail, so I'll just mosey on over and slip him a flask. I won't stay long. Just long enough to let him know that we haven't forgotten him.

See, Mariano went over and visited our so-called leader yesterday, and the damn fool thinks we're going to bust him out of jail. Mariano didn't correct the error of his thinking, and neither will I. Let him think we're just waiting till the time is right.

"Barkeep, how's about you take a bottle of the cheapest, foulest coffin varnish you got in this place and pour this little flask full of it."

Benito smiled at me from his place next to me where we were leaning against the bar. His smile is wide-open and guileless, and leads plenty to believe the man is simpleminded. In a way, I suppose he is. According to Mariano, Benito ain't said a word in all his born days. They come from the same village down south of the border, and they're kin of some sort, cousins maybe. *Primo hermanos*, I think they call it.

It's not so much that Benito is simpleminded, I think. It's just that he don't have no idea about conniving or lying or taking advantage. It's all very basic with him, see. If you tell Benito to do something and he gives his nod that he understands and agrees, it gets done and he just can't imagine how it wouldn't. Which is good, as far as it goes.

Trouble is, he expects others look at things the same way, which of course they don't. And that makes it easy for devious and underhanded types to take advantage of Benito. So he bears watching. Mostly Mariano takes care of that, them being kin and all. But I've got a liking for Benito myself, and so I watch out for him too.

Him not being able to talk just makes people all the more certain he's stupid. I can relate to that myself. It is my natural tendency to keep my own counsel, and I lean toward shyness too, so getting a word out of me ain't all that common. A few drinks will oil up my tongue, though, and just now I'm in a talkative mood—which would be considered taciturn in most men.

The point is, though, not saying much leads folks to believe you ain't thinking much. At least that's my experience. Mostly, I'm just ignored—a stupid old man who ain't got a lick of sense.

That's how Harlow Mackelprang sees me. During our time together, I was just somebody to insult and order around.

"McNulty, once we're in that payroll office, you keep the clerk covered while I empty the safe. And don't screw it up, old man," is how he would talk to me. "Even someone dumb as you ought to be able to handle that."

Or: "Listen, you old fool, I'm the one giving orders around here and don't you forget it. If ever I want to know what you know about robbing stagecoaches, I'll ask. Till then, you just keep your mouth shut and don't confuse me. I'm thinking—which, of course, is something you don't know nothing about, McNulty," he'd say.

And: "You dumb shit, McNulty! I know we didn't get much of a haul off that train—but I gave them folks a good scare, and that's as good as gold in my book. And some of these days they'll be telling their grandkids they got robbed by the notorious gunman Harlow Mackelprang. So you just shut your pie hole and don't forget I'm the one who decides what gets robbed by this outfit and what don't. Dumb old bastard."

So me and Benito were nothing but target practice for Harlow Mackelprang's mouth. Mariano fared a little better, but him being Mexican was enough to convince Harlow Mackelprang that he was stupid too. But he was a little bit afraid of Mariano—as much as a crazy man can be afraid of anything. See, Mariano almost shot him once on account of a dispute they had over some horses that needed to be put out of their misery. Harlow Mackelprang thought it was a waste of ammunition, and Mariano came within about a gnat's eyebrow of wasting more ammo on Harlow Mackelprang.

He wasn't all that sure about me either. He'd seen me skin my old smoke pole a time or two on jobs, so he was aware I weren't no slouch as a gunhand. Fact is, if he had bothered to ask around, which he didn't, he'd of knowed that I had acquired something of a reputation in that line of work. Of course, that was before all this country was crawling with settlers and all civilized and such. Used to be a man could be appreciated for his abilities. Nowadays, they'd as soon lock you up or run you off.

Anyway, since me and Benito and Mariano all kind of sided together, Harlow Mackelprang never quite trusted any of us. I don't think he ever slept with both eyes shut the whole three years we rode together. Especially after he killed Catlin, who had been our leader before.

Hell, we had a good thing going, back before Harlow Mackelprang. I suppose between remembering how good it had been and hoping it would get that good again, we never got around to killing the crazy fool. Now we don't have to bother. He'll be dead enough come morning, and it won't be by our hands—at least not directly. But he'll be dead and maybe things can get back to how they was for me and Benito and Mariano.

I'm hoping that by this time tomorrow we'll be well out into the desert, heading back to that little green valley way out to hell and gone in the middle of nowhere that not many know about. Far as I'm concerned, the three of us can just stay out there forever living the easy life.

Hell, men like us, we can knock over a freight wagon or rob a stagecoach now and then to pick up a little money for supplies. Won't take much, with just the three of us. Maybe we can even convince a wore-out whore to come out there and cook for us and see to our comforts and whatnot. And without Harlow Mackelprang killing people and shooting things up just to get his name in the paper, no one will come looking for us very hard. They'll never find us out there anyway.

The little flask was full, and the bartender screwed the cap on and handed it back to me.

"You sure that's the worst stuff you've got?" I ask him.

"That it is, Uncle. Once I spilled a wee drop of that elixir on me bar and it biled the lacquer clean off."

I tucked the flask into the waistband of my pants and buttoned my old duck jacket to hide it, and gave Benito a wink and started for the jail. Mariano was still parked outside the saloon door where he has been for an hour, leaning against the wall to keep it from tipping over, I guess.

"So Harlow Mackelprang ought to be thirsty about now, don't you think?"

"*Si, amigo.* As I said, the young deputy has taken him the meal. He probably has his snout in the trough by now, snorting like *el puerco.*"

"You think that marshal will let me see him?" I say.

"It was no trouble for me. I think the marshal suspects something, but he does not know what. Just act *muy estupido* and it should go well."

That lawman looked me over good when I stepped into his office.

"What the hell do you want, old man?"

"Well, sir, I was hoping to see Harlow Mackelprang."

"Know him, do you?"

"Used to."

"Who are you?"

"Huh?"

"Your name, old man. What's your name?"

I figured the name McNulty might appear on some reward dodgers, so I wasn't going to give him that. "My name? Oh. Well. My name. Most folks call me McLoney."

"McLoney, huh? You wouldn't happen to know a feller named McNulty who used to ride with that outlaw Catlin, then took up with Harlow Mackelprang, now would you?"

"McNulty? No, Marshal, can't say as I know anyone by that name."

"Funny. His description on some of these posters in my desk fits you right well."

I didn't bother to reply. You don't live to be my age without knowing when someone is trying to trip you up.

"So, Mr. McNulty or McLoney or whatever your name is, what's your business with my prisoner?"

"Just wanting to catch up on old times is all, Marshal. If I don't do it now, I won't be getting another chance, you know."

"I know it. Oh, I know it all right. I trust you ain't armed?"

"No, sir, I ain't," I say as I unbutton my jacket and spread it out so he can see I ain't packing. I know full well, of course, that he'll see the flask tucked in the waistband of my britches. I figure I ain't got nothing to lose—either he lets me pass it on to Harlow Mackelprang or he confiscates it, and whichever one of them drinks that rotgut makes no never mind to me.

Sure enough, he spots that flask and flashes me a look that says he knows what I'm up to and don't care.

"Go on back and see him. I'll be keeping an eye on you."

"Yessir," I says, and heads for the door that connects the office to the lockup. About the time I reach the door, he stops me.

"One more thing," the marshal says.

I turn and look at him, wondering what it is he wants to know now.

"Where were you about three weeks ago?"

"Three weeks . . . let me think. I suppose I was over around Meeker's Mill about that time, seeing if there was any jobs to be had."

"You a mill worker, are you?"

"I'll set my hand to about any job. Long as it's honest."

"Hmmph. I'll bet. You don't happen to know anything about our bank being robbed then?"

"Read about it in the papers, is all. That's how I found out Harlow Mackelprang killed that man and was going to hang for it."

"A man who looks a lot like you do turned in the alarm. That's how we caught him."

"That right? You offer that man a reward?"

"Don't know who he was. He rode away before we could find out. I thought maybe you could tell me who he was."

"No, I don't guess I could tell you that, Marshal," I says.

"No, I didn't suppose you would. Thing is, see, I got a funny feeling that this man and the Mexican he rode away with were in on it. The robbery, I mean."

I wait.

"And I got a feeling that you and one of them Mexicans you been hanging out with over at the saloon might be them two."

And I wait.

"I don't know why, but I think you fellers pulled a double cross on Harlow Mackelprang."

I keep waiting.

"That right, mister?" the marshal asks.

"I ain't got the foggiest idea what you're talking about."

"I'll bet you don't," he says, and starts shuffling through some papers on his desk.

I figure I've been dismissed, so I pass on through the door and see Harlow Mackelprang sitting in his cell on a cot, balancing a tray on his spindly knees and shoving food down his throat like there's no tomorrow. Which, come to think of it, there isn't for him. He's so intent on feeding himself, he hasn't even noticed me standing there. I watch him for a few minutes, then pull out that flask and rattle and bang it between the bars.

That startles Harlow Mackelprang, and he just about jumps out of his jeans, near about upsetting his dinner all over his lap.

"Damn you, McNulty! You always have been dumb as a post and I see your brains ain't improved any in my absence. Fact is, without me around to do your thinking for you, you probably got even dumber."

I just smile and wave that shiny little flask back and forth.

"What the hell you got there?" he asks. "Is that what I think it is? Damn, old man, I could use me a taste of that. You think of bringin' me that all by yourself?" he asks as he sets his tray aside and unfolds himself up off that cot to walk over to the cell door. I pass the flask through the bars and he twists off the lid and throws back a long pull.

The effect is just what I hoped for. As soon as that

flask left his lips, he let loose with a bout of sputtering and spewing. He coughed and hacked for I guess a full minute and more, wiping his running eyes and dripping nose on his shirt sleeve, all the while trying to catch his breath.

"Damn!" he finally says, squeaking the word out like that hanging rope was already squeezing his throat. "That's plumb nasty! Where'd you get that stuff?"

"Just over there at the saloon. Me and Benito and Mariano been drinking it for two days. Guess you just ain't used to it no more, what with being locked up in here these weeks."

Harlow Mackelprang kept up gasping and coughing and dripping out of every hole in his face, still not able to breathe normally.

"You gonna be all right?" I ask him. "Maybe I oughta finish that off for you. You want I should?"

"No. I'll let this settle a minute and try another round. Ain't never been whiskey made that Harlow Mackelprang can't drink."

"You sure? I'd be happy to drink it."

"Sure I'm sure, you old fool. You and them two dumb greasers got a plan to get me outta here, or do I gotta come up with one?" he says as he sits back down and dives into his supper again.

"I have to think of everything," he said around a wad of grub too big to chew. "That's how I rose to the top of this outfit, ain't it?"

"What's that?"

He swallowed a half-gnawed gob. "I said, how d'ya think I rose to the top of this sorry outfit."

"Couldn't say. How?"

"Cream floats."

"Huh?"

"Shovel out your ears, old man. I said, cream floats."

I could barely keep from laughing out loud at that one. But I managed to hold it to a silly grin.

"Well, yeah, sure, Harlow Mackelprang," I said. "But so do turds."

He sputtered out a mouthful of coffee and slopped some more out of the mug when he banged it down on the tray.

"Shut up, you old fool," he said. "Now, tell me. You dummies got any ideas about gettin' me out of here?"

"Oh, don't you worry none," I tell him. "Me and Benito and Mariano been talking it over. Benito, though, he's only been listening, of course."

"So what is it?"

"What's what?"

"The plan, you damn fool! What's the plan?"

"Oh, that. Well we're still working on it. Lots of details to tend to, you know."

"Hell, McNulty, we ain't got all day, you know! They're fixing to hang me come morning."

"I know we ain't got all day," I says with a grin. "But we do got all night."

"Shit! I can't believe my neck's practically in the noose and all I got to save it is you three thick-headed idiots. I'm likely to worry myself to death before they get me hung."

"Aah, well, you won't have to worry too much longer. Just have another drink and relax."

"Relax! You relax! I'm nervous as a whore in church."

"That's why I brung you that whiskey. Drink it. It'll calm you down. And don't talk with your mouth full."

He gives me a dirty look, then takes another pull

on the flask, smaller this time. There's no coughing or hacking; he just screws up his face and squints his eyes, then shakes his face loose.

"Damn! It might calm me down—if it don't kill me. That stuff is nasty. So tell me what you're thinking."

"Well, we thought about stringing ropes through the bars on the window, then takin' a dally and letting our horses pull them bars out."

"For one thing, these adobe walls is a foot thick."

"Yep, we noticed."

"For another thing, the window ain't even in my cell!"

"Yep. We noticed that too. So then we decided to just blow a hole in the wall."

"How the hell you gonna do that, McNulty? These walls is so damn thick it'd take a ton of dynamite to blow 'em and that'd kill me."

"Yep, we thought of that."

"Only way you could do it is get a miner to drill you some holes."

"Yep. We thought of that."

"You idiots! Don't you suppose that'd maybe attract some attention, a bunch of men hiding out in a back alley goin' at the wall of the jailhouse with a steel drill and a double jack?"

"Don't worry, we thought of that too."

"You have any *good* ideas, doin' all this thinkin'?" he asks.

"We thought about maybe just coming through the front door."

"Oh, that's a good one, all right. You wanna know why that one won't work?"

"Why's that?"

"Here's why. Soon as that deputy Charlie gets

back from having his supper and the marshal leaves, the last thing he'll do is lock that big heavy door there behind you and take the key with him. So even if you got through the front door and took care of Charlie, you couldn't get back here. And even if you could bust down them thick planks and get through that door, I'd still be locked in this cell and the marshal will have that key too!"

"Hmmm. We never thought of that, I got to admit."

"Any other bright ideas?"

"Nope. That's it. I guess we'll have to keep on thinking."

"Damn. I'm as good as dead."

"Oh, don't worry. You just watch and wait. When the time comes, I'll give you a sign."

"That's some comfort, McNulty. Some comfort."

He takes another swig of the whiskey; this time it don't seem to bother him none. I guess a feller must build up resistance to that stuff, like they say you do with snake venom.

He turns his full attention to his dinner for a few minutes before saying more. Then: "Tell me something. You always been dumb, or is it something you've learned with age?"

"I can't say I ever thought about it. What makes you wonder something like that?"

"I's just thinking. If getting older means getting stupid like you, dying young don't look half bad."

Right, I'm thinking. If Harlow Mackelprang was to get dumber with age, he'd be a raving lunatic by the time he hit twenty-five—that's if he's twenty-four now, like he says he is. But that ain't nothing he has to worry about now, is it?

"Tell me something else then," he says. "What the hell happened that day we robbed the bank? Mariano ain't nowhere to be found; then when I come out of the bank, you ain't there either."

I thought, how the hell would you know? Soon as you came out that door, your nose hit that wood sidewalk and you wasn't seeing nothing but knotholes. That's what I'm thinking, but that ain't what I say.

"I feel real bad about that. Just one of them things. See, once you two went into that bank, that horse of yours started acting up. He was nervous and hanging back on them bridle reins and snortin' and pawin' and suchlike. Then that got Mariano's horse stirred up and he starts into prancing and dancing around, stirring up the dust, which makes things worse. Then that useless hair bag you been using for a horse reared back, and I lost hold of the reins and he started sidestepping and shying down the middle of the street with Mariano's horse right on his heels.

"Mariano peeked out that bank door and saw what was up, so he came out to help me gather them up. By the time we had 'em under control, you was shooting off that shotgun and the marshal was there and we figured we better just keep on going."

That's the story I tell him. But that ain't what happened.

See, me and Benito and Mariano had all had a bellyful of Harlow Mackelprang. So we more or less goaded him into robbing the Los Santos bank knowing we could queer the deal and get him arrested while we got ourselves off scot-free.

So what happened really was that I dropped the reins of Mariano's horse, ground-tying it in front of the bank while I held onto Harlow Mackelprang's.

Truth is, Mariano's horse wouldn't be a-scared of anything short of a cannon going off if he was harnessed to it. Maybe not even that. About as gentle and well-mannered a horse as I've ever seen, that one.

Anyhow, Mariano followed Harlow Mackelprang into the bank according to the way our idiot leader had set it up.

But instead of waiting there like I was assigned, I rode on over to the marshal's office with Harlow Mackelprang's horse in tow and hailed the law. I pulled my hat down low and screwed my head down into my shoulders so my face didn't show much. And when that deputy what's still wet behind the ears poked his head out, I told him the bank was being robbed and to be careful on account of the robber had a sawed-off shotgun.

Before that deputy could get his wits about him, I headed back toward the bank, and by now Mariano was coming out the door and Harlow Mackelprang was in there hollering and carrying on.

Mariano mounted up and we headed out of town at a brisk pace—not fast enough to arouse suspicion, you understand, but enough to put some distance between us and the fandango at the bank quicklike. We hadn't got far when we heard that shotgun go off and saw that the marshal and that deputy had got there and knew our plan had come off without a hitch.

So we met up with Benito outside of town, where he was keeping the spare mounts for our getaway, just like Harlow Mackelprang planned.

But we didn't need to get away too much anymore, so we just kind of laid low and hung around town waiting to see what happened next. It's amazing how much news a man can pick up just hanging around a saloon minding his own business. Without even asking, we got all the details of the arrest and the trial.

And, of course, we learned the date the sentence was to be carried out, leaving Harlow Mackelprang dangling at the end of a rope too short to reach the ground.

We wouldn't want to miss that.

"Damn, McNulty," Harlow Mackelprang says, jolting me out of my reverie. "That's the same as what Mariano told me. I can't believe you two could screw up a simple little bank job like that.

"On second thought, I guess I can believe it. With a couple of fool Mexicans and an over-the-hill idiot for partners, it ain't no wonder I'm locked up here. Just make sure I'm out of here before morning or I'll kill all three of you sorry bastards. You hear me?"

"I hear you. No need to get upset. Don't you worry none. Like I said, just watch for my signal."

Here's how that's going to work, I think as I leave the jail.

Tomorrow morning, when the legendary gunman Harlow Mackelprang climbs them thirteen steps to the top of the gallows to where he can get a good look at the crowd, he'll see me and Mariano and Benito sitting out there just past all the town folks on our horses.

And when he sees me, I'll grin at Harlow Mackelprang and give him a thumbs-up.

"What a stupid thing to do," he'll maybe say to himself. "I wonder what he means by that."

HENKER

Harlow Mackelprang's last supper, while substantial in quantity, will not add appreciably to his weight. A few ounces perhaps, but not enough to require adjustments to the usual formulas for a hanging, which determine the length of drop required to snap the neck cleanly.

The greater problem with the man, I think as I contemplate him through the bars of his cell, is the fact that he is as long as a polygamist's clothesline and not much bigger around. A decided disparity in the usual relationship of height to weight.

I judge the man to be just shy of six feet and three inches in height. But he is so skinny, I doubt he would tip the scale at more than a hundred and fifty-seven, maybe fifty-eight, pounds. Just figuring in my head, that weight wants a drop of, say, eight foot ten inches, or maybe nine foot even.

This will require some consideration. Frankly, it is going to be more difficult than I thought, and will require that I check the gallows again.

Allow me to explain. A nine-foot drop is not unusual

in a hanging. I myself have dispatched a number of miscreants at that distance, as weights of a hundred and fifty-four to one hundred and sixty-eight pounds are common. The average man, you might say. The corresponding drop ranges from the aforementioned nine feet down to eight foot eight, depending.

But this "average man" with whom I am well acquainted usually stands well under six feet in height—three or four inches less, say. And oftentimes, a man with a stocky build will achieve that weight at five and a half feet. Even shorter.

You see my problem.

All this, within ten seconds of Harlow Mackelprang's rising from his filthy cot and standing before me, fills my mind.

In my early years in the hanging trade, it would have taken considerably longer to arrive at this point. Not to mention a carefully balanced scale, a measuring tape, and referral to the charts and graphs from England. But long experience and a practiced eye allow me to forgo those mechanical devices and calculate the death drop of the ne'er-do-well in the instant.

Fine adjustments—an inch or two—are often required based on the structure of the criminal's neck, and this always—always—requires a thoughtful analysis. I fear that Harlow Mackelprang's death will be complicated even further by this variable.

Aaah, the life of a hangman.

Perhaps you think, as many—nay, most—do, that hanging is a simple matter of wrapping a rope around a man's neck and shoving him down a hole or hoisting him up to draw it tight. Oh, that will kill him all right. Eventually.

But conducted improperly, a hanging becomes an unpleasant, agonizing affair rather than the quick dispatch of a death sentence. And only the most cold-hearted among us demand a nasty and painful death to satisfy the requirements of justice.

That "quick dispatch," then, is my trade. One I came by honestly and have practiced with pride these twenty-six years.

Twenty-seven years ago, I arrived in this country from my childhood home along the Rhine River. Lacking skill in the English tongue, my options of obtaining a livelihood in America were limited.

I had served an apprenticeship as a printer in my homeland. But again, my lack of ability to read or write the American language disallowed employment in the composing room as I could not, of course, set type. Oh, I could have made my way, I suppose, performing other tasks as I learned. But the printer's ink that had blackened my fingers throughout my younger years did not flow in my veins, and my desire was for something different.

The Army, in those days and even now, offered a haven for the immigrant. The duties required of the enlisted man were simple and easily explained with a few words and gestures. So I found myself in uniform as a private soldier, assigned to the frontier post Fort Custis.

"Henker!"

Sarge had a nasty habit of shouting in one's ear to scare away sleep. I was immediately upright in my bunk, blinking and wondering why. It was still deep darkness.

"Yessir?"

"Roll out and report to the stockade."

"Stockade? What have I done?" I asked, now frightened as well as disoriented.

Sarge laughed. "Not a damn thing, Henker. At least not yet. But you're about to do something. One of the guards over there, Knopfler, has took sick. You're his replacement. Get a move on."

Thus my introduction to law enforcement.

Knopfler did not recover from his illness, as it turned out, and was buried a week later. My duty as a stockade guard became permanent. Among my charges was a fellow named Walser. He too was recently arrived in America, and his boyhood home had been not far from mine. We knew our friendship would be brief, as he was locked up for killing a comrade. The other soldier had cheated him at a gambling game and Walser, in a drunken rage, beat him to death with an oaken barrel stave.

To shorten a long story, Walser was sentenced by the court-martial to hang and I was on guard duty when the sentence was executed.

Military hangings were not public affairs. They were not exactly hidden, understand, as that would interfere with their function as a deterrent to crime. But neither were they festive occasions as civilian hangings often are. At Fort Custis, hangings were rare and the officer in charge of the stockade was responsible for their administration. Walser's hanging was the first there for more than two years.

With the usual military precision, the trapdoor was set, rope strung from the gibbet, and Walser marched to the gallows to the rat-a-tat of snare drums. With the usual military ineptitude, the trapdoor jammed, breaking Walser's fall.

All of us on duty watched, shocked and sickened at

the sight of Walser trussed up like a turkey, convulsing and gagging at the end of the rope. It occurred to none of us, standing there fully armed, to put the poor bastard out of his misery with a gunshot or even the thrust of a bayonet, either of which would have been preferable to the officer's course of action.

What the officer-cum-hangman did was this.

Walser was bobbing at the end of the rope, several feet below the officer's station at the trip lever atop the gallows. Recovering from his initial shock at the malfunction of the gallows, he walked the few steps across the platform to the trapdoor and gazed down the hole.

He then grabbed the rope with both hands and slid down its length. His descent ended when his feet hit Walser's shoulders, and he proceeded to jump up and down there in an attempt to break the soldier's neck. The sergeant of the guard then joined the action, running under the gallows and wrapping his arms around Walser's legs and pulling downward.

Eventually—it seemed hours, but must have been but a few minutes—Walser's convulsions ceased and he was declared dead.

In the officer's defense, he was as shattered by what had occurred as the rest of us who witnessed the catastrophe, if not more so. He informed the commanding officer that, should occasion demand another hanging, he absolutely would not perform the duty, and that an experienced executioner should be brought in for the distasteful task.

Occasion did demand another hanging, as it turned out, just four months later. An Irishman named Callahan forced his intentions on a washerwoman, whose determined refusal led to a violent beating from which she died. Callahan, whose fond-ness for drink and ungentlemanly behavior had kept him at the bottom of the ranks despite his many years of service, was sorry for the woman's death.

But he did not consider the fault his own, believing the availability of sexual favors on laundry row was his—and every soldier's—due. His defense boiled down to: "Everyone knows that's why we have washerwomen—this laundry business is nothing but a sideline. Had the woman done her duty, she'd not be in the fix she's in."

The court-martial did not see it his way, however, and sentenced him to hang.

True to his word, the officer in charge of the stockade refused the duty. Seeing his point, the post commander sent off to a military prison seek-ing assistance.

Dunn answered the call.

A proper Englishman, Dunn was a military officer, but had little use for the trappings of the service. He saw his duty as executing miscreants, performed his duty with perfection and enthusiasm, and ig-nored all else.

As a matter of fact, Dunn walked a fine line, con-tinually in danger of being charged with insubordi-nation for ignoring superior officers, failure to properly attire himself in military uniform and re-galia, and exhibiting near-total disregard for proto-col in all its forms.

But give the man a gallows, a length of rope, and a death sentence, and his efficiency and proficiency weighed so heavily in his favor that all else was coun-terbalanced. Dunn would hang men singly or in groups, adolescents or the aged. He would hang women. He would hang soldiers or Indians, officers or enlisted men. And he hanged them all with a smile on his face.

I fell under Dunn's spell the first time I saw him. He breezed into the stockade one afternoon, all bluster and business.

"Take me to the prisoner Callahan, lad," he demanded of me.

"State your business, sir," I replied, unsure of the "sir" as he was only partially in uniform and his status uncertain.

"I intend to kill the man. Now stop the nonsense and take me to him or stand aside."

"I don't understand, sir."

"I am the executioner, you daft lad. The hangman. I demand an audience with my man. Now hop to it."

"Yessir," I said as realization dawned. "This way, please."

I led Dunn upstairs to where Callahan was locked up, and even though I was moving at more than double time, his feet on the steps dogged mine, their impatience hurrying me along even faster.

"This is it, sir," I said, stopping before a cell door, like all the others, made of heavy dark wood with a small rectangular hole cut through at eye level.

"Unlock the door. I have to see my man."

"Yessir. But watch him, sir. He's not in the best of moods lately."

"Don't you worry, lad. I shall not be intimidated by any common criminal. Especially an Irish ruffian.

"Callahan!" he shouted as I swung the door open. "On your feet!"

"What the hell do you want?" he asked, blinking in the sudden light.

"I want to put a noose around your neck and hang

you until you are dead. It shouldn't take more than a minute. I stand ready to do my part. Do you?"

"Are you giving me a choice then?" Callahan said.

"Only whether you will face it like a man or like a whimpering Paddy."

"Damn the disgrace. My death not only comes on account of a Mexican whore, but at the hands of a bloody Englishman."

"You would do well to thank your lucky stars for that, Callahan. Despite the deficiencies of your heritage, professional pride requires that I dispatch you in an instant with neither pain nor suffering. You'll be burning in the depths of hell before you even know what has happened. Now, turn around." Callahan turned his back to Dunn and stopped.

"Keep going," Dunn said after a few seconds.

"You stand five feet and eight inches, I say, and weigh twelve stone and three."

"You're right with me height. But you'll have to tell me pounds for I don't know 'stone' from shit."

"Twelve stone three makes you one hundred and seventy-one pounds."

"Right you are, last time I checked."

"Now, Callahan, I must have a feel of your neck. It will take but a few seconds."

"My neck? What in hell for?"

"To determine the strength of the musculature, identify any injuries, check for irregularities of bone structure. All in a good cause, I assure you. Steady on."

Dunn then grasped Callahan by the neck and probed and squeezed and stroked with all eight fingers and both thumbs. He asked Callahan to tip his head from side to side and again turn in a circle as he examined the neck from all angles.

"My God, man," Dunn said, "you've a neck like a Durham bull. Thicker than your head and just as hard."

"I don't suppose that's cause to spare me as an unlikely candidate for hanging, is it?"

"No, no. No indeed. Just another inch or two added to the drop. No matter how strong your neck, it will snap like a stick of kindling because your falling body is stronger, you see. Strictly speaking, you will kill yourself when hanged. I am merely the instrument that brings it about."

"Some comfort, that," Callahan said.

"Until we meet again then, two mornings hence. Buck up," Dunn said as he turned and left the room. By the time I locked the cell and took the stairs three at a time, he was already well across the parade ground.

"Mr. Dunn, sir," I called.

"Yes?" he said, looking back at me with a curious stare. I hustled over to where he waited.

"If you don't mind my asking, sir, what will you be doing next?"

"I intend to take a late breakfast at the officers' mess, then get settled in my quarters and perhaps nap for an hour or two before examining the gallows."

"Mind if I help you, sir?"

"With which function—the meal or the nap?" he asked with a twinkle in his eye.

"No. I'm sorry, sir. Pardon me. With the gallows— the hanging."

"Hanging's caught your fancy, has it, lad?"

I explained the hanging of Walser, and the distaste it created for shoddy workmanship due to lack of skill. I told him that even though Walser had been something of a friend, even my worst enemy deserved a better fate than the one he suffered.

And I told him his examination of Callahan had indeed caught my fancy and I wanted to learn more of his methods.

"I should be delighted to have your assistance," he said. I had the feeling from his enthusiastic agreement that not many people expressed an interest. I found out later—both from Dunn and from my own experience—that not only do hangmen fail to arouse interest among the mass of mankind, they are more often shunned and despised.

"I shall request—demand actually—that the post commander assign you to me as assistant executioner throughout the duration of my stay."

"Thank you, sir."

"Don't thank me yet, lad. You may regret those words later. Save your gratitude until the hanging is accomplished and see if you still wish to express it then."

That afternoon we—he, I should say; I merely hung over his shoulder—checked the gallows from the bottom of the pit to the top of the gibbet. A pair of carpenters had been detailed to Dunn, and he outlined a series of tasks for them, shimming up the platform to level it, reinforcing the joints on the gibbet, and replacing warped planks on the stairway.

The offending trapdoor was removed entirely, and Dunn demanded the carpenters smash it up on the spot. He sketched out plans for a replacement, and sent the carpenters to the shop to see to its manufacture.

We next visited the blacksmith shop, where he ordered the smith to forge a new set of hinges and bolts and a trip mechanism. Despite the protests of the smith that the work would take three days to accomplish, Dunn demanded it be finished in twenty-four hours with the threat of court-martial if he failed. I had already discovered that while Dunn had no use for military protocol, he did not hesitate to use his rank as a weapon in order to force his will.

Long into the night and all the next morning, Dunn schooled me in many aspects of the hanging art—which is what he considered the task.

"It is a science in many ways," he said, "requiring mastery of engineering, mathematics, physics. But a hangman must also be a philosopher, moralist, and mystic. The combination of such disparate skills is indeed an art, lad."

He related the ways and means of hanging in England, where the most advanced techniques and methods were developed and are continually refined.

"There was a hangman in Yorkshire, Mr. Berry he was, who reasoned out the number four hundred and twelve—an otherworldly number that forever changed hanging. It is a simple and elegant solution to calculating the length of drop.

"Simply divide four hundred twelve by the condemned's weight in stone, and you have it. Accurate to within an inch, as simple as that. A major breakthrough which saved untold grief and suffering on the one hand and blood and gore on the other.

"It doesn't work, of course, here in the colonies where weight is no longer measured the English way. While no one, to my knowledge, has arrived at an American equivalent to Mr. Berry's magic number, I have developed conversion charts that serve me well. It is unfortunate, though, that as in so many other ways, American imitations are but crude facsimiles of their English counterparts."

We talked of rope, and the superiority of three-quarter-inch, five-strand Italian hemp. He showed me how to soften the fibers and make the rope more pliable and lively by rubbing in gun oil. He told of the advantages some perceived in a metal ring with a leather keeper over the traditional hangman's knot, but allowed that he preferred the thirteen-coil knot for symbolic reasons, if not functional ones—for he personally believed the added force of the coils snapping the head aside at the point of impact contributed to a cleaner break.

He showed me the proper method of tying the hangman's noose—getting the proper twist in the coils, the proper tautness, the proper appearance. He demonstrated its placement, with the knot set just at the angle of the jaw on the left side of the head in order to achieve the proper sideways jerk. It was important to Dunn that everything be "proper."

And he regaled me with tales of hangings gone bad because of an "improper" approach. The stranglings, like poor Walser suffered, where a body can struggle for five minutes or more before the life is choked out of it. These, he said, are the result of insufficient drop.

And he told me of the opposite problem—too long a drop. He had witnessed botched hangings where the extreme force of the drop snapped the head right off the body, leaving the head to bob in the noose while the body poured blood into the pit, often spraying bystanders.

I confess fascination with it all. I cannot explain its appeal. Perhaps it was the fact that I was able, from the beginning, to separate the humanity of the hanged from the technique of the hanging. I do not know. But it seemed to me then, as it still does, that it was a job that needed to be done and it deserved to be done well.

Upon delivery of the new ironwork and woodwork to the gallows, Dunn directed the installation of the new trapdoor. His improvements in the mechanism were immediately obvious. The trip lever slid the bolts with silken smoothness and the hinges allowed the door to fall as freely as if it were unattached. Dunn repeatedly applied lubricant to the bolts and hinges, wiped them clean, and applied a different type of oil or grease in an effort to find one which performed flawlessly. I was satisfied long before he was.

Then the oiled rope was anchored and looped around a bag containing exactly one hundred and seventy-one pounds, as measured on the sutler's scale, of a mixture of sand and lead shot. Dunn dropped the bag through the trap several times, exactly eight feet and eight inches.

"You have to stretch your ropes, lad," he told me. "A fresh rope, see, has a bit of give in it. Hang a man with it and the stop isn't so sudden—it stretches a bit when it hits bottom so some of the energy of the drop is directed into the rope rather than the victim's neck.

"Snapping the neck cleanly between the second and third cervical vertebrae requires a striking force of twenty-four hundredweight. That's the purpose of all the tables, you see. But if the rope stretches, it absorbs some of the force and you're back to strangling the man, even if you've calculated the drop correctly."

Once the rope was properly stretched, the bag stopped dead at the end, with nary a bounce nor bob, merely a low-frequency twang and resounding hum. Dunn stopped immediately, declaring the rope perfect and not wishing to weaken it with further tests.

The hanging of Callahan was accomplished without a hitch. And I was hooked.

My assignment as Dunn's assistant was made permanent, pending approval from up the chain of command, which was granted. I accompanied him back to the military prison and served as his assistant for a period of two years and four months and thirty-three hangings. Dunn was satisfied with my performance and declared that he had taught me all he knew, and that experience only would improve my abilities.

When my term of enlistment was up, I opted to leave military service and ply my trade as a hangman in the civilian world. The work has been steady, satisfying, and lucrative. I have never wanted for money and can work on my own terms. The expertise I learned at Dunn's feet has served me well.

I have enjoyed the privileges of travel. My work takes me to city and town, from the civilized East to the barely tamed West, from sultry Southern climes to wind-whipped Northern winters. I have visited deserts so arid they dry the saliva right out of your mouth, and witnessed the deadly force of hurricane-driven rains.

I have moved about by horseback and buggy, stagecoach and freight wagon, and spent more hours and days and weeks and months on the move than I could remember even had I been sober. With the advent of the modern rail network, I seldom find myself at any great distance—in terms of time—from any assignment I choose to accept. But the travel is still extensive, as much by my choice as circumstance.

Among the benefits of that choice is the satisfaction of having sampled the wares of countless breweries in many cities, enjoying the malt beverage within sight of the place of its birth. Likewise, the wares of whiskey artisans across the country. The velvet smoothness of grain alcohol fresh from the oak aging barrel at the distillery bears no comparison to the adulterated slop served from bottles in saloons and roadhouses. But the traveling man takes what he can get.

While my line of work has provided many advantages, it has, at the same time, been a living hell.

In my apprenticeship, you see, the cloak of protection offered by the military shielded Dunn and myself from the malice of civilian society. But upon leaving the service and ever since, I have found myself a social outcast.

Mothers shoo their children out of my presence like a hen driving chicks away from a serpent. Men, save a few wishing to satisfy a morbid curiosity, carry their drinks to the opposite end of the saloon. Passengers on trains and coaches select seats as far from me as possible once they learn my identity. Even harlots, let alone decent women, resist consorting with me.

Were it not for drink, my life would be a lonely one. Even with the comfort of drink—perhaps, to some degree, because of drink—I have grown bitter.

You see, while I never did care a whit for the men I kill, I have learned over the years to likewise despise the men who pay me to do it and the crowds who gather to watch. I laugh in their faces, treat them

Rod Miller

rudely, hang their criminals, take their money, and drink straight from the bottle through it all.

If they wish to consider my presence a necessary evil, I will do nothing to change their minds.

I have grown less careful in my calculations over the years—not careless, mind you, merely less careful. It has all become routine, so to speak, and requires little in the way of serious thinking.

The challenge of Harlow Mackelprang is a welcome diversion.

"Step over here, Harlow Mackelprang," I tell him.

He stops just across the bars and I reach through and encircle his neck with my hands. That gets the attention of the young deputy leaning on the doorpost, and he snaps to as if awakened from a bad dream. Once he is made to realize that all is well, he drifts back into his daydreams.

"I see you have had a little something to drink," I tell the prisoner as I palpate his neck muscles.

"What of it?"

"Nothing. It pleases me. I enjoy a good drink myself, and am not one to begrudge any man the pleasure. In fact, in these circumstances, I often recommend it. Have you any more?"

"A little. Only had a hip flask to begin with and I guess I've drunk half of it."

"Might I suggest that you save the rest until morning? A good stiff drink before hanging will oftentimes allow even a lowly cur like you to stand on the gallows with a little dignity."

"Don't you worry none about me. I won't give the people in this town the pleasure of seeing me snivel."

"You are a big talker, Harlow Mackelprang, but I know your type. I suspect your willpower is as weak as your skinny neck. So you just save that whiskey for morning and save me the effort of dragging you kicking and screaming up the gallows steps."

I explained the procedure we would follow come morning.

The marshal would shackle and handcuff him in the cell and lead him under guard down the street to the gallows. I warned him there would likely be a crowd and he would be forced to run a gauntlet of insults. I would meet him at the bottom step of the gallows and lead the way to the top. The preacher would be waiting there to offer up a prayer, if wanted.

The Marshal too would climb the steps, leaving the armed deputy at the bottom to keep the crowd at a respectful distance.

"Once we are up there and alone in the wind, Harlow Mackelprang, it is best just to get it over with. Pray with the preacher if you so choose. The marshal will read out the legal papers about the hanging. You will be invited to speak if you wish. I shouldn't bother if I were you, because no one gives a damn what you have to say.

"Walk to the mark I have made on the trapdoor and face the crowd. I will bind your ankles tighter than the shackles do, with a length of rope. I will check the security of your hands in the handcuffs behind your back. Do you understand?"

"Yeah, I get it. Don't sound like much to me."

"Good. Then I will place the noose around your neck and draw it snug. I will place a soft cloth bag over your head. You will hear me walk a few steps across the platform. By the time you realize I have stopped walking, I shall have tripped the lever and you will be dead. Do you understand?"

"I suppose so. You've done this all before, ain't you?"

"Indeed I have, Harlow Mackelprang. It has been a good many years since I have hanged a man who has killed more men than I have."

"Shit. I wished I'da known about your line of work. I do enjoy killing folks."

I laughed at that one. "It does have its pleasures. Especially when you consider that I never have to kill innocent people—just low-life murderers, rapists, sodomites, gunmen, and other vile criminals like you who don't deserve to breathe the same air as decent human beings."

He laughed at that one. "I reckon you've got a point there. Only I don't agree about decent folks. All the ones I have ever seen have been as worthless as me, if not worse. I can't hardly stand to be around them."

"We shall free you from that burden come morning, Harlow Mackelprang. Let's get it done and over with in a hurry so I too can get out of this godforsaken town."

With that, I left him. I walked down the street to the gallows and calculated the distance from the gibbet to the ground. Harlow Mackelprang's lack of bulk required a long drop, see, and I had to assure myself that the extreme length of the man would not hit the ground before he hit the end of the rope.

On the other hand, there's that damn skinny neck of his. It's likely to stretch right in two if I drop him that far. I guess there's nothing to do but curl up in my hotel bed with another bottle of whiskey and give it some serious consideration.

You see my problem.

ALTHEA

Harlow Mackelprang's last supper echoes forth in a foul-smelling belch that fills the room like a creeping miasma.

A revolting display of his utter lack of manners. It is not my first exposure to the man's lack of couth.

Thank God it shall be my last.

In my line of work I see men at their worst. As often as not, I see the worst of men. I submit, without fear of contradiction, that Harlow Mackelprang is the lowest of the low, the absolute nadir of humankind, residing on the underside of the bottom of the deepest hole.

And I have seen a lot of men. A lot.

I will not mince words, although I shall attempt a socially acceptable description of my occupation. I am a fancy lady—or as near as you will find of the type in Los Santos and for many miles in any direction therefrom. A woman of ill repute, if you would rather. I entertain gentlemen (using the word advisedly) in my home as a commercial proposition. Am I clear, or shall I go on?

Let's call it good.

It has been an interesting enterprise. Not one I came by honestly but one that, once thrust upon me, proved so lucrative relative to the effort expended that I could not envision a change of career.

I will relate some of those details in time, but first allow me to say why I am here; why I have made the effort and taken the trouble to call upon Harlow Mackelprang in his jail cell on this, the eve of his execution.

The explanation is simple: I want to spit in his face and invite him to enjoy an eternity in hell as penance for the wrongs he has committed against my person.

"Harlow Mackelprang, is that any way to greet a lady?" I say.

"Why, Althea," he says, obviously startled at my presence at his place of incarceration, "you are a sight for sore eyes. But you sure ain't no lady."

"Mind your manners. I can leave as easily as I came, you know."

"I reckon that's true enough. What brings you here? You fixing to comfort me in my final hours?"

"Don't be morbid. And don't be silly. If you were perishing of thirst and I had the only libation on earth, I would refuse to moisten your tongue."

"I'm not sure I followed all them fifty-cent words, but I take it that's no."

"Not just no, Harlow Mackelprang. Hell, no!"

"Why Althea, listen to you curse!"

"I have not begun to curse you."

"I always thought we were friends, Althea."

"You have never been my friend. I have put up with much abuse from men in my life. But seldom have I been treated in the vile manner in which you treated me."

My "involvement" with Harlow Mackelprang commenced a good many years ago and coincided, more or less, with the arrival of his physical manhood. In a town the size of Los Santos, my means of earning a living is not a secret. This knowledge results in sidelong glances from men, total disregard on the part of their wives, and insatiable curiosity among adolescent boys. Most are satisfied to giggle and whisper upon sighting me.

Harlow Mackelprang, however, wanted more. His curiosity surpassed insatiable and became an obsession. For a number of years, I seemed to attract him like a magnet during my every foray into the town. At first he kept his distance, content to stare at me from afar and, I swear, drool. As he grew older and became bolder, his proximity on occasion became oppressive. While inspecting goods in the stores I might turn and trip over him, as he would creep close enough to sniff my perfume and stealthily stroke the fabric of my garments.

Contributing to the discomfort of the situation was his size. Harlow Mackelprang was tall for his age, surpassing many grown men in height. To find him unexpectedly towering over me was intimidating and discomfiting.

The unpleasantness was compounded by his personal grooming—or lack thereof. His clothing was always ragged and dirty. His body was unwashed. His hair likewise, and uncombed as well. His skin pimpled and pus-laden. It is a mystery to this day why I could neither catch his disagreeable odor upon his approach nor escape from it once he was gone.

At times while entertaining gentlemen callers I would, for lack of a better term, "get the willies"— the odd, anxious feeling of an unseen presence or of being watched. As you have no doubt guessed by now, it was because I *was* being watched. By Harlow Mackelprang, as he lurked outside my windows. I can imagine the education he received thus, and cannot bear to imagine the self-gratification it may have involved on his part.

Fearing for my safety and that of my customers, as well as the loss of business that would result should this lack of privacy become known, I petitioned the marshal for help and protection. I felt entitled, having paid his "assessment" on my business promptly and regularly on the tenth of every month for the duration of my presence in Los Santos. (In addition to providing the occasional "favor" to the marshal himself or an out-of-town associate he wished to impress and entertain.)

But to no avail. Not that the marshal did not believe me. And not that he did not attempt to remedy the situation. But Harlow Mackelprang had, and still has, I suspect, a sixth sense that warns him when trouble approaches. That sense, combined with the boy's practiced stealth in moving about the town and concealing himself, meant the marshal was never able to catch him in the act of peeping Tomery—or whatever other acts that might accompany it. The marshal even confronted Harlow Mackelprang about it directly on a number of occasions, and the boy merely scoffed at my accusations and his warnings.

I believe he eventually outgrew his reprehensible

behavior of that ilk. But what was to replace it was, in the end, immeasurably worse.

To begin with, Harlow Mackelprang stopped skulking around outside my windows—I believe—and started knocking on my door. He must have been about eighteen years old at the time. I must admit his personal grooming had improved with maturity. Still as long and skinny as a beanpole, he at least bathed and shaved on a somewhat regular basis.

Nevertheless, I refused to admit him to my parlor.

No matter how often he came around or how much he begged, Harlow Mackelprang was not allowed over my threshold. He feigned politeness at first. But on occasion he would grow angry at my intransigence and throw a temper tantrum. Other times he would whine and snivel like a spoiled child. In all that time, over a period of two or three years, he never laid a finger on me, nor did he threaten violence.

So why would I not invite him in? Women in my line of work are not known for being picky. We take what comes and take their money and take who's next as long as it's there for the taking. We take men who are hairy and men who are bald, men who have bathed and men who should have, shy men and boisterous men, nervous men and men who haven't a care in the world, men who are violent and mean and, rarely, men who are tender and kind. They are all men and it is all work and it is all money.

It is work that is seldom pleasant or enjoyable. Usually it is barely tolerable. You must learn to give a man the pleasure he seeks no matter what is involved or what is asked. Many women of my kind turn to alcohol or opium to insulate themselves from the harsh realities of the work. I simply close my eyes and mentally count my money. That is the strategy I have found most useful to ensure personal survival.

So why did I not take Harlow Mackelprang's money?

I have asked myself that question over and over again. Perhaps if I had taken his money, things would not have spiraled downward into the bloody, vicious, sadistic well that later engulfed me.

But every time I have asked myself why, I have wanted even more to ask Harlow Mackelprang why. This is my last chance and I intend to take it.

"Why did you do it, Harlow Mackelprang?"

"Why'd I do what, Althea? Hell, I done a lot of things."

"Why did you force your way into my parlor that night, then force yourself on me?"

"That's the business you're in, ain't it? My money's as good as the next man's."

"But it is *my* business. *I* decide who I will and will not entertain, and whose money I will and will not take."

"But why? Something wrong with my money?"

"Don't ask *me* why. I am here to ask you."

"Hell, you know, Althea. I was young and full of myself and figured I was way past due for havin' me a woman. Since all them prissy little honest girls around town turned up their noses at me, you were the only chance I had. And you are in the business. It ain't like you were choosy until then."

"I told you no."

"Aw, shit, Althea. How dumb do you think I am? I ain't takin' no from no whore."

"But you hit me."

"Damn right I did. Like I said, no wasn't goin' to cut it."

"I had an unsightly mouse under my eye and bruises and discoloration on my arms and chest. How was I supposed to keep working in that condition?"

"Everything seemed to work fine to me," he says with a cruel laugh.

Once again, the utter repulsiveness of the man engulfs me like a stained sheet, as it has so often in the past.

"I meant my other gentlemen callers, Harlow Mackelprang. Not you."

He laughed again. "Gentlemen? That what you call them? Is that what I am, Althea, a 'gentleman caller'?"

"Nothing, I mean nothing, could be further from the truth. The words 'Harlow Mackelprang' and 'gentleman' are contradictory. So why did you do it? Tell me why."

"Like I said, you had what I wanted and I meant to get it. Truth is, though, it wasn't as good as I thought it would be. But slappin' you around—I *liked* that. Got me all stirred up inside, if you know what I mean.

"Hell, if it wasn't for you getting me all mixed up, I likely wouldn't have got all mad and shot that cardsharp in the saloon or busted up the place. But you had me howlin' at the moon, Althea."

Another belch, the equal of the original in stench and foulness, rolls out of Harlow Mackelprang. Then he continues.

"And, of course, if'n I hadn't of done that, I wouldn't of done all that other stuff—you know, setting fire to the stable and robbing and shooting that stupid dirt farmer. Then I wouldn't of thrown in with Catlin and become a bandit and gunman."

Now it was my turn to laugh. "I see. So it is I who must bear responsibility for all your misdeeds."

"I ain't sayin' that. But you don't know how it is with a man."

"Harlow Mackelprang, you are the world's ultimate fool. I know more about 'how it is with a man' than you will ever know. Or have you forgotten whence comes the money that supports me?"

"Hell, no. How could I forget? That's why I kept coming back."

"I surely wish you had not."

"What, come back?"

"As I have said, I wish you had not darkened my door the first time. And I wish you had never darkened it again. Your visits were the worst thing that ever happened to me."

"Well, I sure enjoyed coming to see you. I never thought you liked it, but I never knew you didn't neither."

"I hated it. I hated every minute. You are so crude and vulgar. Breaking into my house in the middle of the night, unannounced and uninvited. Striking me with fist and foot. The cuts. The bruises. The pain. The swelling. The blood. How could you possibly think such treatment could be anything but hated? I despise you for it!"

"I paid you, Althea. Paid you right handsome every time."

"In the first place, if you will recall—supposing your puny brain has sufficient capacity for a modicum of memory—on many an occasion you offered no payment whatever, merely a request that I charge it to your imaginary account. But even when you left cash behind, it did not count for payment. I never kept a cent of your tainted money. Not a penny of it, Harlow Mackelprang. It all went to the poor fund at the church. Every cent."

"Then alls I can say to that is you're a damn fool."

"That I am, Harlow Mackelprang. I wouldn't feel nearly so foolish today had I but shot you dead. Fortunately, that will not be necessary now. Your death will not come at my hand, but it will be no less satisfying. I cannot wait to see you hang."

"I don't know, Althea. You'll be losing a customer. At your age you can't afford to be losing customers, can you?"

If I could reach him through these bars, his demise might come at my hands after all. But I swallow the impulse, determined to remain calm. But it is not easy, given his observation.

It is all too true, sad to say. I have reached "a certain age." In my line, that age comes earlier than it would, say, for a bank clerk. (Which, incidentally, is a career about which I made inquiries upon the death of Calvin, the clerk killed by Harlow Mackelprang three weeks ago and for which he hangs in the morning. Despite my patronage of the bank over the years and the sizable nature of my deposits there, Tueller, the manager, rejected my entreaties. He did not believe the good people of Los Santos would accept the presence, in a place of legitimate business, of a woman with my reputation.)

Much of my clientele is regular and loyal and, given the lack of competition, likely to remain so. But I will not have the wiles to attract the younger element as I once did. A young man will ride a goodly number of miles for the company of a young woman, even if it is a commercial proposition.

In my time, though, young men were as a moth to my flame.

I was blessed with a luxuriant black mane, so thick and rich and lustrous in its color that it reflected highlights of red and blue. My skin, by contrast, is a radiant milky white, smooth and silky and free from blemish. Dark brows frame large eyes with a tempting catlike slant and irises that sparkle and dance with a deep, glowing shade of green.

These gifts—and gifts they are, for they are not of my making—have necessarily faded some with the years, but are still with me in sufficient quantities to attract the admiring glances of men and the appraising, envious looks of women. Women, even, of fewer years than mine.

My appearance, if modesty allows, remains striking. And whatever I have lost with age is more than compensated for by the increase in confidence and grace that comes with experience. In sum, I am as yet more than qualified for this work in every possible sense of the word.

But, as I indicated earlier, I did not come to this work by choice. It was thrust upon me in an hour of desperation while I was in a depressed state of mind. I was but seventeen years old; newly married and recently widowed and far, far from the security of my childhood home and the protection of my family.

Mine had been a privileged existence, daughter of a wealthy Crescent City merchant. My introduction to society at the coming-out age of sixteen was a round of balls and parties, with eligible bachelors from the best families pursuing me.

But I scorned their advances and, much to the displeasure of my parents, became enamored with a young man of the West.

He, like my father, was a merchant. Except that Owen was engaged in the grimy business of overland trade to the settlements in the Southwest, rather than the more genteel world of overseas shipping in which my father labored.

He was a customer of my father, and that is how I met Owen. Much to my family's chagrin, I abandoned the promise of Crescent City society and ran off in the night with Owen. My father, of course, knew Owen's route and destination and itinerary and could have located us and attempted to force my return. But the shock and hurt, I think, combined with the blow to their pride, would not allow it. So, I was convinced, they simply wrote me off as a bad investment.

Our "honeymoon" was an idyllic journey through the countryside. Owen had come alone to Crescent City, preceding his wagon train of trade goods from the West to establish markets for his wares and bargain for merchandise for the return trip. My first encounter with Owen was at our dinner table. Father had been in negotiations with him that day, and invited him to dine at our home so discussions could continue into the evening.

It was a tumultuous occasion. Never had another human being aroused such strange and confusing feelings. None of the eligible bachelors who crowded my social calendar that summer were memorable or particularly attractive.

But from the moment I laid eyes on Owen, I knew

I had found my man. Much to my satisfaction, the feeling was mutual.

I am aware that my account sounds like breathless entries in a schoolgirl's diary. I do not mean to make it so. And the fact that my parents discouraged us only encourages comparison to storybook romances recounted in purple prose.

But the fact is, Mother and Father were less than sanguine at the prospect of a daughter doomed to life on the frontier in the company of a man who was little more than a mule skinner or bull whacker. So, after a week of near-continuous companionship, we were denied further contact.

We were not to be denied, however, and as I said, stole away in the night.

We camped in the woods, late each afternoon locating a likely location well off the roads. Owen was a master at rough living, and had all the accoutrements required for making the experience as comfortable as possible. We retired early and arose late, lingering over simple meals and traveling unhurried in a westward direction with no schedule to keep. Our passion for one another did not diminish, but rather grew until we became insatiable.

But after a mere two weeks of bliss and serenity, I was sucked into a bloody maelstrom of murder, rape, and abduction.

The men came from nowhere. Three of them rode out of the dark forest into the glow of our fire. We had finished a simple dinner and were preparing for bed. I will remind you that we were but two weeks man and wife. And we considered the seclusion of our campsite sufficient cover for our immodesty. We were mistaken.

Owen stood to greet our visitors when, without word or warning, all three riders revealed pistols and shot him down.

To make a long and painful story short, the men took their turns with me repeatedly through the night. In the light of dawn, they plundered our supplies for what they found useful, broke up the light wagon, and heaped our discarded goods into a funeral pyre for my Owen.

One mule from our team was designated a pack animal and I was forced to mount the other. I was an accomplished equestrienne, but prior to that day, when I was forced to ride astride, my experience on horseback was confined to a sidesaddle on gentle, well-trained, blooded horses. Of intransigent, rough-gaited mules I was ignorant.

Residual pain and soreness from the night, combined with the unaccustomed means of riding, resulted in a most uncomfortable day that stretched into a week.

My captors rode aimlessly, it appeared, throughout the land. Their mood was celebratory, due to their newfound wealth at Owen's expense.

A seemingly endless supply of strong drink, replenished by one of the men riding out periodically to visit whatever community was convenient, heightened their delight in their excesses and contributed to my misery from same.

Eventually, they tired of me.

I was dumped unceremoniously early one evening into a fetid alley behind a gilded palace of shame in the city (so called) of Rio Mal. I was not found until morning, when stumbled upon by a drunkard who had sequestered himself in the alley the night before to sleep it off.

There was not much of me to find. The ordeal had left me a mere husk of myself. Hungry, thirsty, bruised, bleeding, smeared with filth inside and out, I was carried to a room in the brothel.

I wish I could say a kindly, good-hearted madam nursed me back to health and helped me get my life back in order. Instead, the woman who owned the place grudgingly fed me and allowed the use of the room until I was up and about, then demanded back payment of rent. Knowing I was penniless, she fully expected repayment through trade, and thus her stable grew by one.

I was an attractive addition, I might add, increasing the popularity of the place and fattening madam's purse. By the time my debt was satisfied, she offered—begged actually—to keep me.

It was a dilemma I did not care to face. As the Bard of Avon wrote, there's small choice in rotten apples.

But still, a choice was required of me.

So, did I return to Crescent City, a widow and fallen woman at seventeen, to throw myself on the mercy of my parents and society? Or did I accept the offer of a lucrative career in Rio Mal, trading used, damaged goods for any coin offered?

My state of mind at the time—disgusted, disgraced, damaged, depressed—led me, almost by default, to the latter choice.

And so my life was set on a course not of my choosing, albeit by my choice. For nearly a quarter of a century now I have been, in the parlance of our time, a painted lady.

The road I have taken since Rio Mal has led to cow

towns and mining camps, railheads and river landings, cities being born and towns in their death throes. I have, as I said, known more men than I could (or would care to) count. I have performed acts that would make you blush and have done distasteful, disgusting, revolting, and abhorrent things.

I located in Los Santos some ten years ago, drawn by the mining activity in the distant hills and the presence of the railroad. The location of Los Santos is such that it is assured of commercial activity so long as the trains run, the mines are profitable, and people have a taste for beef.

While it is not likely to flourish, it is likewise unlikely to founder. I opted to abandon the boom-and-bust nature of the communities in which I had normally plied my trade for the relative stability and quieter environs available here.

In the process of my work in Los Santos as well as my earlier relocations, I have accumulated, as I hinted earlier, a good deal of money—I tell you that not in my defense but only in explanation.

But, I should add, not all my wealth has come from my work. Having been raised with money and privilege, I was not entirely ignorant of the workings of the capital markets. Thus, my investments have proved lucrative. As I said before, my holdings in the Los Santos bank are sizable enough to set the bank manager's spectacles spinning.

He doesn't know the half of it. Or even a tenth.

Since my age will soon necessitate the cessation of my trade, my wealth will provide a more than comfortable retirement. But the idea of inactivity is unattractive. (More, even, than working—if you can imagine.) I cannot envision pulling up stakes to settle elsewhere as a "respectable widow," which is the usual fate of women in my position.

But employment in Los Santos seems out of the question. One thing I have always enjoyed about life in the West is the willingness of people to ignore the past and accept people for what they are or claim to be. But when a sizable portion of your past has been lived out right under their noses in their own community, it cannot be overlooked.

So I suspect I shall have to leave Los Santos soon and seek work elsewhere. That my employment needn't be gainful, and I require only that it be interesting, may prove an advantage.

The idea of banking, as I said, intrigues me. Perhaps I could read for the law and practice in the legal profession. If a worthy community could be located, I fancy that I might even establish and operate a lending library or bookshop.

I have not decided, and I need not decide today. The only thing I must decide at present is how to put Harlow Mackelprang in his place and extricate myself from this unpleasant situation with pride and dignity intact.

Which became exponentially more difficult when I realized that while I was lost in thought, he had come to stand at the cell door and mere inches separated us. Worse still, one of his filthy hands had slipped through the bars and was toying with the lace at my throat.

"Harlow Mackelprang, remove your squalid paw from me this instant!" I shout, simultaneously shoving the offending appendage aside with all the violence I can muster.

The tender part of his wrist strikes the iron bar

with some force, prompting an outcry of pain and an attempt to withdraw the hand. But the slim distance between the bars and the resulting lack of mobility it creates makes my puny strength sufficient to hold him there, the wrist bound between the pressure of the bars and my hand.

I lean on it vigorously, plying sufficient leverage to cause the coward to snivel and squirm.

"Damn! Leggo my hand, Althea! You're hurting me!"

"Do not presume to speak to me of hurt, you obnoxious swine."

With that, I perform a most unladylike act—I clear my throat and expectorate explosively into his face.

His sniveling turns to surprise, then anger. He rises to his full height and thrusts his other arm through the bars in an attempt to grab me.

I avoid his grasp without much difficulty and continue grinding his pinioned wrist against the iron.

More by instinct than forethought, I jab my furled parasol between the bars and strike him in the groin, causing him to give up all fight and collapse to the floor. I release his hand, which slowly scrapes its way out of its bind, allowing him to complete his fall.

Seeing the villainous gunman lying there, writhing in pain and whimpering like a whipped dog, I experience a change of heart.

I will not attend the execution in the morning as I no longer care to see Harlow Mackelprang hang.

I prefer to remember him just as I see him now.

PREACHER

Harlow Mackelprang's last supper, from the smell of things, was washed down with coffin varnish. Like brimstone raining down from on high, the stink of whiskey leaks out of his every pore.

The man is beyond redemption.

And judging from the fact that he mopped the plate clean of all but a few scraps, gluttony may be added to his lengthy list of sins.

Sloth as well. Just look at him laying there on that cot like he ain't got a care in the world—and him with an appointment with the hangman come morning.

"Harlow Mackelprang, arise," I command.

He stirs, casts an evil look my way with one half-open eye, then swings his feet over the edge of the cot and sits. After grinding the heels of his hands into his temples for a few seconds, he speaks.

"Good hell, preacher man. Can't a man get any sleep around here?"

"Bridle your tongue. I have come to prepare you to meet your Maker."

"You're too late. Reverend Hangman's already been by and done that."

"He has his duty. I have mine. I see you had a big supper."

He offered no reply.

"And I detect you have been at the devil's brew, on this of all nights."

"So what? Another few hours it ain't gonna matter how much I ate or drank."

"'For the drunkard and the glutton shall come to poverty and drowsiness shall clothe a man with rags.' Proverbs, Chapter Twenty-three."

"What?"

"You are guilty of drunkenness, gluttony, and sloth, Harlow Mackelprang. All sins in the eyes of the Lord. For a man about to go before the judgment bar, I should think you would have tried to avoid further contamination of your soul."

"Oh, that. I thought, from what you said, I oughta be worried about becoming poverty-stricken on account of my habits. I figure I can risk that for these few hours."

"Do not quibble over the Lord's words. It is your spirit that is poverty-stricken, your soul that is clothed in rags."

"Whatever you say. You're the Bible-thumper, not me," he says.

"Do not scorn that which is holy. Familiarity with the Good Book might have turned you from a life of crime."

"Yeah. Just like it did all them folks lined up in your pews of a Sabbath morning. They ain't as pure as you think."

"It is not them that I am here to discuss, Harlow

Mackelprang. It is the fate of *your* immortal soul we should be concerned with, not theirs."

Again, no response.

"Are you resigned to your fate?" I ask.

"You mean hangin'? I don't guess I'll be any less dead afterward than them I killed are. Oh, I'll be killed all legal-like and proper, but I'll be just as dead."

"Such is the law. Both in the eyes of man and the eyes of God."

"You know what he sees, do you, Preacher?"

"It is written. It is plain for all who have eyes to see. 'Thou shalt not kill.' Book of Exodus, Chapter Twenty. You have violated that law. 'And he that killeth any man shall surely be put to death.' Leviticus, Chapter Twenty-four. So you see, God himself has declared that you must die."

"Well, at least when I do, it'll all be over with."

"No, it will not. You will suffer for your sins. You will burn in hell for eternity for the evil you have done."

Even that failed to evoke fear or trembling. He sat upon his cot slack-jawed and droopy-eyed. It called to mind his attitude those few times he came to church, bored and wishing nothing more than for it all to end.

I suppose it has been two decades since old Broom showed up in Los Santos with Harlow Mackelprang in tow. I made a pastoral visit once they were settled into the shack that was to be their home. Rather than making it a home, though, the two of them made it a hovel.

Broom's story was that his wife, the boy's mother, died of pneumonia a couple of years earlier. Then a mine injury rendered him incapable of work. He admitted to being in the grip of alcohol and unable to shake loose. I wrote him off on the spot as beyond redemption.

But I held out hope for Harlow Mackelprang.

He could not have been more than five or six years old at the time. For a few Sundays, I called faithfully at the shack to take the boy to services. He was neither willing nor unwilling; simply did as he was told.

His father was seldom in at the time, either swamping out the saloon or some other business. When he was present, he was all in a heap with his filthy blankets in his louse-infested bed sleeping off the effects of his chosen profession, that of drunkard.

The boy came along to services, as I said.

He had no clothing appropriate for worship. Not that fancy dress was the norm in Los Santos. Many in the congregation had only simple, well-worn attire, but it was generally laundered and fresh each Sabbath morning. The boy, however, had only rags, and filthy ones at that. None of the children would share a pew with him, and adults shied away as well.

So he sat alone, at the end of the front bench directly below the pulpit.

Close though he was, the word of God never appeared to reach the boy. He fidgeted and napped and never heard a word. After a few weeks, maybe a month or two, I realized the futility of the effort and stopped calling around for the boy, and he did not attend anymore.

Oh, he did show up a time or two about the time he became aware of lust. I noticed him slipping in late on a few occasions and lurking at the back of the meeting room, positioning himself for the best view of the blossoming young girls of the town, then slipping out again before meeting's end.

His reappearance at the church under those circumstances, I felt, called for another visit to talk with Harlow Mackelprang and his father. I waited and watched, and one day saw Broom on the way to his shack early in the afternoon appearing at least somewhat in control of his faculties.

A quick reconnaissance of the back alleys of the town turned up the boy attempting to reason out the operation of a tobacco pipe, but having no luck in keeping it lit. I, of course, confiscated the paraphernalia of sin on the spot, breaking it up and tossing the pieces, along with his twist of tobacco, into the dung heap behind the livery stable.

"Hey! What the hell you do that for?" he asked.

"Watch your mouth, boy. A tool of the devil, Harlow Mackelprang. That's all that evil weed is, a tool of the devil. Where did you get it?"

"Found it."

"Stole it more likely," I said. "'Thou shalt not steal,' the Lord God commands."

"Don't make no never mind, one way or t'other. You got no call to throw it away."

I did not pursue the subject, having other irons in the fire. "Come along, boy. We're going to see your father."

He laughed, then said, "You think he's gonna care that you caught me smoking?"

"That is not why we are going. Just come along."

"Supposing I don't want to."

That did raise a question. Although he could not have been more than thirteen years old at the time, he was already approaching me in height—and I am six feet tall.

Still, he was a boy, and an impertinent one at that.

So I slapped him hard with my left hand, then grabbed a handful of his cheek with my right and gave it a good twist. Much like a twitch on a horse's lower lip, this tends to take a boy's mind off rude behavior and sassiness, if only temporarily.

"I did not ask if you wanted to, Harlow Mackelprang. Now let's go."

By the time we were out of the alley and in the street, I figured he was tamed for the time being and turned loose from his face.

"Damn!" he said, rubbing the insulted cheek vigorously. "What you wanna do that for?"

"Tame your tongue, boy, or I will do it again."

He offered no more sass for the remainder of the trip, merely shuffled along half a step behind me, murmuring.

We arrived at the shack just as Broom came out the door.

"Well, Preacher," he said. "To what do I owe the honor?"

"We need to talk. About your boy."

Broom eyed the boy suspiciously. "What's he done now? I swear, boy, you don't shape up, one of these days I'll take a strap to you."

Broom's bloodshot eyes turned to me. "So what's he done?"

"He has been showing up at church services."

"I should think that would please you, Preacher." Broom laughed. "Give you a chance to save a soul. God knows, his needs it."

"Don't blaspheme, if you please, sir," I warned. "It

is not his presence that I object to. It is the reason for his being there, and his behavior."

With that, Broom lowered himself slowly onto the overturned powder box that served as the shack's front step, propped his elbows on his knees, and laced his fingers behind his bowed head.

"What's it he's done?" he asked, the question muffled by his position.

"A better question might be what he intends to do. The boy is consumed by lust. He prowls around the back of the meeting hall like a herd bull waiting for the cows to come in season. I swear, I have seen him curl his lip and sniff the air."

Broom dropped his hands and raised his red eyes to meet mine.

"That's it? That's all? You dragged him home to tell me that? Hell, the boy's coming of age. Happens to everybody."

"It is different with Harlow Mackelprang. He makes the girls nervous. Their parents too, of course. I have had reports that he is likewise lurking about the school. The marshal has had complaints that he peers in windows at night.

"It is part of man's fallen nature, as you imply, to lust after women. But the Lord expects us to bridle our lusts and passions and not succumb. The commandments say, 'Thou shalt not commit adultery,' and, 'Thou shalt not covet thy neighbor's wife.'

"I fear the boy is consumed with lust and has it in mind to violate those sacred commands if he has not done so already, whether his partner is willing or not," I told Broom. "And I will warn you that several of the fathers in this town are keeping their eyes on him. They will not hesitate to act if they feel their wives or daughters are threatened."

Broom mulled this over for a time, then said to the boy, "What you got to say for yourself?"

The boy said nary a word, his eyes burning with hate, his face flushed with embarrassment.

"Speak up, boy," Broom said.

Still, the sin-riddled boy seethed in silence. Almost involuntarily, my right hand dealt him a sharp backhand slap to the face.

I shouted, "Pay attention, boy! Honor thy father."

As my mark on the boy's cheek reddened to a deeper shade than the angry flush on the rest of his face, Broom cast a penetrating glance in my direction that left little doubt that he would not countenance further assistance of that sort from me. He turned back toward his son.

"C'mon, boy. Speak your piece."

"I got nothing to say. Not nothing."

"You been bothering any girls or womenfolk?"

"No."

"You got it in mind to?"

"No."

"You best not. I hear anything more, I'll turn you into a steer. You got that, boy? You know what I mean by that?"

Harlow Mackelprang did not reply. His shifty, hateful gaze lashed out at Broom and myself in turn. The threat, extreme though it seemed, accomplished its purpose. The boy backed off and, so far as I know, never approached any of the town girls in an inappropriate manner.

Not that they stopped worrying that he might. When encountering the boy on the streets, the mothers of Los Santos gathered their budding daughters into the folds of their skirts as hens gather their chicks.

Girls walking unescorted, or in the company of their friends, were often seen crossing streets or ducking into convenient doorways to avoid encounters with Harlow Mackelprang.

Even grown women wrapped shawls tighter about their shoulders and hurried past Harlow Mackelprang with heads down and eyes averted. It seems the fairer sex shared an aversion to the boy as if he were afflicted with the pox or some other evil contagion that might spread through the most casual contact.

And so the lust and wicked desire accumulated with his age, fed by anger and indignation at every slight. I felt it my bounden duty and sacred call to see that his pot did not boil over to the ruination of the females of my flock.

His pent-up rage was relieved many years later, I am told, upon the harlot Althea. She, being engaged in the practice of such an evil and wicked trade, deserves whatever punishment Harlow Mackelprang chose to mete out.

Now, these many years later, he sits before me as unrepentant as ever, the threat of damnation and the wrath of God having no effect, even as he faces death.

"God will punish you for your sins. You know that, don't you?"

"I figure he might give me a break."

"Highly unlikely," I scoffed. "'Cursed be he that taketh reward to slay an innocent person. And all the people shall say, Amen.' Deuteronomy, Chapter Twenty-seven.

"'He is an holy God; he is a jealous God; he will not forgive your transgressions nor your sins.' Joshua, Chapter Twenty-four."

And then I heard another voice.

"'Come now, and let us reason together, saith the Lord. Though your sins be as scarlet, they shall be as white as snow; though they be red like crimson, they shall be as wool.'"

The words of Isaiah surprised me with their appearance in that den of sin. I turned toward their source, the darkness of the corner cell. "Who said that?"

"God himself. Book of Isaiah. First chapter, eighteenth verse."

"I know *that*. Who are you?"

"A sinner. 'For all have sinned, and come short of the glory of God,'" the voice said.

"Romans, Chapter Three," I replied. "And that is true. We all are sinners."

"Aah, yes. But contrary to what you have been saying to Harlow Mackelprang, all is not lost. There is hope. Read in Deuteronomy, Chapter Four, where it says, 'For the Lord thy God is a merciful God; he will not forsake thee, neither destroy thee.'"

"But this, from Psalm One Hundred and Four: 'Let the sinners be consumed out of the earth, and let the wicked be no more.'"

"I answer from the Twenty-third Psalm," he said. "'Surely goodness and mercy shall follow me all the days of my life and I will dwell in the house of the Lord forever.'"

The man troubled me with his interpretation of Scripture. "You have read the Good Book, it is clear.

But methinks your interpretation of its message is not the same as mine."

"That does seem obvious, doesn't it, Preacher."

"You never did tell me your name."

"Sweeney. Not that it matters."

"I am curious, Sweeney. How do you come to pervert the Holy Word so? Such a thing is not to your credit"

"Whatever do you mean?"

"Allow *me* to quote from Isaiah. Fifth chapter. 'Woe unto them that call evil good, and good evil; that put darkness for light, and light for darkness; that put bitter for sweet, and sweet for bitter! Woe unto them that are wise in their own eyes, and prudent in their own sight!'"

"So you think that I quote Scripture to support evil then, is that it?" Sweeney said.

"Yes," I said.

"In what sense?"

"Your abuse of the Word will give Harlow Mackelprang false hope. It is abundantly clear in Scripture that retribution is required, that evil must be recompensed. As in Exodus, Twenty-one. 'Thou shalt give life for life, eye for eye, tooth for tooth, hand for hand, foot for foot, burning for burning, wound for wound, stripe for stripe.' I could go on, as I am sure you know, Sweeney."

"And I do not doubt it, Preacher. But surely you have read the Apostle Paul's Epistle to the Romans, where he clearly states in Chapter Twelve, 'Recompense no man evil for evil,' and, 'Avenge not yourselves, but rather give place unto wrath: for it is written, Vengeance is mine; I will repay, saith the

Lord.' Are we not presuming the Lord's role in taking vengeance on Harlow Mackelprang?"

"Perhaps. But I think not. I quote from Numbers Thirty-five. 'The murderer shall surely be put to death.' More to the point, Genesis, Nine. 'Whoso sheddeth man's blood, by man shall his blood be shed.'

"By *man*, it says, Sweeney. By man. I take that to mean that God has not only given us the right to act in His behalf in these matters, but the responsibility."

"And who is worthy to take upon himself the role of God?"

"What do you mean?"

"As Jesus Christ himself said to a self-righteous mob much like yourself, 'He that is without sin among you, let him cast the first stone.'"

"I will cast aside vengeance then. What about retribution? Do we not have a right to demand retribution of those who do wrong? Surely the Bible tells us so."

"I am of the opinion, Preacher, that your Bible-reading is too much restricted to the Old Testament."

"The ancient prophets are to my liking, I confess."

Sweeney says, "My preference is for the New Testament, where I find more hope."

"But hope does not relieve you of responsibility."

"No. But even you hellfire-and-brimstone preachers cannot completely ignore the story of the Savior Jesus Christ. The first chapter of Ephesians speaks 'to the praise of the glory of his grace, wherein he hath made us accepted in the beloved. In whom we have redemption through his blood, the forgiveness of sins, according to the riches of his grace.'"

"Grace is a troublesome topic. I would not want my eternal salvation to rely on it," I say.

"'And he said unto me, My grace is sufficient for thee, for my strength is made perfect in weakness,' Second Corinthians, Chapter Twelve," he replies.

"There is certainly merit in what you say, Sweeney. But you forget one important thing—all that you say applies to believers." I turn my attention from the dark depths of the cell Sweeney occupied and back to the condemned. "Are you a believer, Harlow Mackelprang?"

"Sure, I'm a believer. I believe lots of things. I believe the both of you is full of shit."

"Is there no end to your vileness? Are you wicked to the very core?"

"Beats the hell out of me, Preacher. What do you think, Sweeney? Is there any hope for a low-life ol' gunman like Harlow Mackelprang over here?"

Sweeney didn't respond for a moment, thinking it over. Then: "You are worse than you think, Harlow Mackelprang. And worse, I fear, than anyone else imagines."

That drew a snorting laugh from Harlow Mackelprang. "I thought you was on my side, Sweeney," he says. "It's bad enough I got this Bible-thumper in a long black coat and boiled shirt down on me, without you piling on."

"I am neither hot nor cold, neither for nor against," Sweeney says. "I am merely stating my opinion. Although I doubt he would see any benefit in such action, perhaps you should confess your sins to the preacher."

"I won't do no such thing," Harlow Mackelprang says.

"What's your point, Sweeney?" I say.

"All will soon be revealed, Preacher," he says.

Then: "Harlow Mackelprang, do you understand the nature of sin?"

"Sure I do. I ain't stupid, you know. That's when you do something bad to somebody that don't deserve it."

"And do you believe you have ever committed a sin?" Sweeney asks.

"No, sir, I don't."

That certainly gets my dander up. "Harlow Mackelprang, you are an admitted thief, a robber, a rapist, and a murderer! And now I see lying can be added to the list! Just seconds ago you said you were not stupid. How can you deny that you are a sinner?"

"I never did nothing to nobody that didn't deserve it. In my life, I took a lot more than I ever dished out."

I cannot believe what I am hearing. "What about young Calvin, over at the bank? What did he ever do to you?"

"That little sissy was just like all the others in this town when I was growing up. He'd cross the street just to avoid walking past me. Besides, he worked at that bank. Them crooks cheated me out of a wad of cash one time. Claimed I never give it to 'em and I couldn't prove they did on account of they never gave me one of their little books. I only wished I'da had time to burn the place down after I robbed it and shot Calvin. I shoulda shot that damn Tueller while I was at it."

"But it was cold-blooded murder!"

"He had it coming."

"How about Soren? Did he have it coming?"

"He sure as hell did. That dumb dirt farmer wasn't going to give me the loan of his worthless plow horse."

"Loan! You were stealing the horse!"

"Same thing," he said. "I needed a horse. My life was in danger. Ain't a man's life more important than an old horse?"

"I could ask you the same question."

"Well, I'da give it to him if he needed it."

"But he did need it. It was his means of livelihood."

"Yeah, but he coulda got another horse later. I had a damn posse breathin' down my neck."

"Harlow Mackelprang, I cannot believe what I hear." The man really did think he was an innocent, a victim.

"What about that woman at the inn up at Madera? I know you'll claim her husband, Murphy, and that lodger harassed you into killing *them*. But what did that poor woman do?"

"Hell, she was married to Murphy, wasn't she? I just used her to get to him. And I damn sure did, I'll tell you. Besides, I never killed her. She didn't come to no harm."

"You raped her!"

"Oh, that ain't nothing. She mighta even liked it if she'da relaxed a little."

Such indifference to the sanctity of life and the dignity of God's children is astounding. I find myself stuttering and stammering, unable even to respond to the machinations of such a sick and distorted mind.

Sweat trickles down my ribs, whether from the heat of the anger within or the proximity of the flames of hell, I cannot say. As is often the case when I am at a loss for words, I fall back on the word of the Lord.

"But you have clearly violated the most basic of God's laws. Thou shalt not kill. Thou shalt not steal. Thou shalt not commit adultery. Even you have heard of the Ten Commandments. I do not doubt you have broken them all. You are a sinner, Harlow Mackelprang, of the worst kind. Worse even than that, you are an unrepentant sinner."

He makes no reply.

"Were I in your shoes just now, Harlow Mackelprang, I would be quaking."

"I don't doubt it, Preacher. But you're a coward and I ain't."

"You, no coward! You are the worst kind of coward, preying on the helpless and those you have rendered defenseless. We will see your so-called bravery as you approach the gallows come morning. I will enjoy watching you whimper and snivel.

"Even more, I would like to see how brave you are an instant after you hit the end of the rope and find yourself face-to-face with your Maker. You will stand at the judgment bar and I prophesy you will be found lacking! Fear the Lord, Harlow Mackelprang! Fear the Lord!"

"Can't say as I do. Fact is, I'm sorta looking forward to meeting him."

"Looking forward?"

"That I am, Preacher. And when I do meet him, I'll spit right in the old gentleman's eye," he says.

"Blasphemy! On top of all else, you are blasphemous and profane. Were I not so angry and were you not so unrepentant, I would pity you. But I feel only hate."

"Not very Christian of you, that."

"Do not presume to speak to me of the things of God or Our Savior Jesus Christ. I shall now shake off the dust of my feet and remove myself from your presence. Should you have a change of heart and wish a prayer in your behalf come morning, I shall do my duty. Otherwise, Harlow Mackelprang, may you burn forever in hell."

Without further ado, without even bidding Sweeney (whose arguments I found stimulating, if misguided) farewell, I leave the jail. I need to fall on my knees and repent of letting that spawn of Satan get the best of me. I am guilty of anger, unkindness, incivility, even outright hatred.

I feel I have faced a devil, and now a devil is within me.

Harlow Mackelprang's accusation of an unchristianlike attitude sits heavy on my soul. Only his complete depravity and sinful, unrepentant nature counterbalance these twinges of guilt. I believe in my soul of souls that the man is beyond help. Beyond redemption even. And I can think of but one thing to do:

Pray for Harlow Mackelprang.

On second thought, I shan't bother. He won't appreciate it. It will waste my time. And God might be insulted.

BROUSSARD

Harlow Mackelprang's last supper consisted of beefsteak with gravy, mashed potatoes, beans, sauerkraut, biscuits, peach cobbler, and coffee. He took the meal in a six-foot-by-eight-foot cell in the jail at Los Santos, where he was held for three weeks, two of which while awaiting trial and the other while awaiting the execution of his death sentence. His trial . . .

No.

Decked out in duck trousers, Texas boots, a soiled dress shirt without cuffs or collar, and a striped vest, Harlow Mackelprang took his last walk this morning. Accompanied by the marshal and a deputy, both heavily armed, the gunman walked the block and a half down Front Street in Los Santos to the gallows. . . .

No.

The West today rid itself of its most notorious bandit, the murderer Harlow Mackelprang, in a public hanging in the city of Los Santos. Arrested here three weeks ago and tried and convicted a week ago for murder and bank robbery, the execution marks the end of a three-year reign of terror

during which the gunman Harlow Mackelprang
and his outlaw band robbed, rustled, raped, and
murdered their way across the territory. . . .

Not that either. Maybe this: Blood and horror
earned their due today. The citizens of Los Santos
repaid erstwhile resident Harlow Mackelprang for
the shotgun murder of a bank clerk with public
hanging. The execution draws the curtain on a
three-year crime spree. . . .

No. It will not serve. Here I sit on top of the
biggest story ever to come out of Los Santos, the one
story likely to propel me out of obscurity and into
the rarified air of top reporters on daily newspapers
with a nationwide audience, and perhaps an opportunity to reshape my tales for the crime maga-
zines published in the East, and I cannot come up
with a suitable lead.

For nearly two and a half years I have toiled for the
local weekly in the employ of one Mr. Ford, splitting
my duties as a reporter with setting type, proofing
galleys, composing advertisements, and even assist-
ing with the press run. It is not the situation I desire,
but one I am told I must endure in order to learn
the business and gain the experience necessary to
advance.

Which may be true, I suppose. But "learning the
business" is not something I care to do. I have neither the desire nor the inclination to operate a
newspaper. My sole purpose is to be a reporter—
a writer actually, with literary pretensions, and the
reporting is merely the means by which I acquire the
material to be written up.

But it is difficult for one to make his mark and
arouse the interest of distant editors in one's abili-

ties when the subject matter of one's stories is confined to mining shipments passing through, market prices for cattle, the arrival and departure of relatives visiting the notables of the community, recent occurrences with the ladies' horticultural and literary societies, and the like.

To be honest, the one bright spot since my arrival here has been Harlow Mackelprang.

Interest in his activities due to Los Santos being his hometown, as well as the proximity of his crimes (combined, I must add, with a nearly total lack of other notable events in the territory hereabouts), have afforded an opportunity for me to follow his exploits through dispatches from and to area law-enforcement authorities, rewriting stories from other newspapers, and even, on a few occasions, traveling to other communities to gather information firsthand.

One such excursion, taken just a week and a half ago, in the days leading up to Harlow Mackelprang's murder trial, took me to the Meeker's Mill mining district in the mountains. That, it was said, was the place of the bandit's birth, infancy, and early childhood.

By journeying there I hoped to fill in some gaps in the general knowledge concerning our local gunman's origins, information about which was sketchy. I admit my purpose had little to do with my stories for readers of the local newspaper. They cared little about the outlaw, feeling—with some legitimacy, I suppose—that they already knew more than they wanted to about Harlow Mackelprang, man and boy, and the course of his young life before it upset theirs mattered not a whit.

No, my hopes were more related to the possibility of peddling an account of the life of Harlow

Mackelprang to the publishers of dime novels or, perhaps, legitimate biographies.

And so I bought a ticket and boarded the train for Meeker's Mill. The speed of train travel has its advantages for the journalist. But for one with literary ambitions it can prove a liability.

How, after all, does one get a sense of place when thundering through it at breakneck speeds approaching thirty miles per hour?

How does one absorb the smell of sage, the delicate odor of rain curtaining from a summer thunderhead, or the hint of campfire smoke on the breeze, when one is overwhelmed with the acrid stench of burning anthracite and the putrid proximity of dozens of unwashed fellow travelers?

How, in the midst of such pounding and pulsing, huffing and whistling, can you expect to detect the distant cooing of a mourning dove in the gray dawn? The rhythmic chirp of crickets concealed in the gloaming, or coyote calls relayed through the darkness on moonbeams? Or even the annoying clatter of locusts in the noontime sun?

And what of the clear air of the West, which can distort fifty miles of distance into what appears a mere hour's ride on horseback? That too is lost when traveling by train, as everything you see in every direction wavers and warps, dims and deforms through a haze of coal smoke and ashes stirred by an artificial wind.

But as writers are wont to do, I have wandered too far from the subject at hand. So allow me to pick up the tale of Harlow Mackelprang at the place of his birth—the mining area known as Meeker's Mill.

Gallows frames topping numerous mine shafts

marched up and down the sides of a steep, narrow canyon. At the mouth of the defile, sprawling across the only flat piece of land of any size, stood the mill works for which the area was named—the focal point of which was a noisy stamp mill that pounded and pulverized ore at any and all hours of the day and night.

The rails ended just short of the mill works. The train station consisted of nothing more than a six-by-six shack holding a pigeonhole desk and sheet-iron stove.

Beyond, a switching yard allowed railroad workers to shuttle cars to and from the tipple for loading, then assemble them into a train with the passenger cars for the trip back down the mountain to Los Santos and points onward.

Limited as it was, rail service to Meeker's Mill kept the mines thereabouts considerably more active and prosperous than their counterparts in the neighboring Thunder Mountain district. There, mule-drawn freight wagons hauled ore and supplies, stagecoaches hauled people and mail, and the bone-rattling wagon road they all used was the only means in or out.

One result was that the commercial traffic on the Thunder Mountain road from Trueno to Los Santos offered a more tempting target for bandits like the late Catlin and soon-to-be-late Harlow Mackelprang. A stagecoach or freight wagon is considerably easier to stop than a train.

But again, I digress.

An inquiry at company headquarters—a shoddy two-story affair of rough-sawn lumber—garnered no information.

"How long ago?" the chicken-necked clerk asked, peering down his long nose at me.

"Twenty years, more or less. Can't say exactly."

"Boy, you have any idea what miners are like?"

"Like everyone else, generally speaking, I guess."

His snort turned into a condescending laugh; then he said, "They're like a bunch of damn gypsies. That's why they call them 'gyppo' miners. They move from job to job and place to place for any reason or no reason at all. Twenty years would see more hundreds of miners than you can count coming through here."

"But this man was married. Had a family. I just thought that might have kept him here a little longer."

"Might have. Even so, anyone that might remember him is probably long since gone."

"How about payroll records?"

There was that snort again. "I've been keeping the books here for twelve years. Had he been here during that time, there might be a chance. The records before then are a hopeless jumble. Couldn't find anything even if I wanted to."

"So you won't help me."

"Can't."

"And you don't think anyone would remember them? None of the miners, or their families?"

"What's the name again?"

"Mackelprang."

"Well, that's not a name you hear every day. Could be somebody might remember it, if you can find somebody that's been around that long," he said. "You might try over in Mechanicsville. That's where most of the workers with families live. But there ain't many of them. Like I said, most of what we get here are footloose gyppo miners."

A nondescript place, Mechanicsville. Not a proper town, it was but a double row of ramshackle huts, cabins, shacks, and wood-walled tents occupying an unwanted side canyon a hundred yards downhill from the mill.

A few questions and a little nosing around led me to a whitewashed house halfway up the neighborhood's one street. Its white walls were the only color in the canyon that showed through the film of dust that covered everything, and the only wood of any hue other than the natural drabness of aged, untreated rough lumber.

"Mackelprang, you say?"

"Yes, ma'am," I replied, attempting to encourage the old woman with the tone of my voice. Grayhaired and wrinkled, she was as weathered and worn as everything else in the canyon, but still as neat and tidy as her cottage.

"That's a long time ago. But sure, I remember them. They moved in that little place two doors down right after they married. Lot of folks have lived there since. But they came to mind a year or two ago when I started reading about that outlaw Harlow Mackelprang in the newspapers. Knew it had to be the same boy.

"A right ambitious housekeeper, that Bonnie was. Made a real nice little home of that place. She and I, we neighbored some while they were here. Things started going bad, though, once she took sick and succumbed.

"That baby boy never had much of a chance after that, once his dad took to drinking so."

I asked if anyone else might still be around that would remember them.

"You go on up the street, clear to the end, and there on the right you'll find a place that looks to be a junkyard. Woman there used to look after Harlow Mackelprang once his mother Bonnie passed.

"Now I'm not one to tell tales, young man, but were I you, I would decline the offer of any food or drink at that house. Of course, I've not heard of her offering."

Stacks of warped and weathered boards, rusting metal, boxes, and all manner of detritus littered the dooryard of the house I was directed to. Glass was missing from more windowpanes than not, haphazardly replaced by ill-fitting scraps of board. Tin cans hammered flat, covered others, as well as patching what must have been holes in the shack's lapboard walls.

Picking a path through piles of trash and refuse, I made my way to the door and knocked. I tracked the progress of someone inside by the squeak of floorboards, so was ready, with hat in hand, when the door swung and rattled wide on loose-fitting hinges.

At least I thought I was ready.

The woman filled the doorway. Greasy hair and fabric hung and clung to various parts of her person. Every expanse of exposed skin sagged and bagged, from jowls to arms to ankles. Even her lower lip seemed to surrender to gravity, its droop revealing a single brown tooth, thrusting upward at an unexpected angle.

I was speechless.

She did not speak.

I found my voice eventually, at least some of it,

clearing my throat and spilling out a collection of syllables only marginally coherent.

"Excuse me. Harlow Mackelprang. Do you know him?"

She stared at me through drooping, dripping eyes, clouded with a film of ignorance.

"What?"

"Harlow Mackelprang," I repeated. "Do you remember him?"

A glimmer of recognition appeared in her rheumy eyes.

"What for you want to know?"

"I'm from the newspaper. He's going to trial for murder in Los Santos. We're just looking into his background. For our readers."

From behind the woman came the unmistakable sound of the cocking hammer on an unseen weapon. The type of weapon soon became clear as an ancient, oversized percussion-cap pistol in a hairy, white-knuckled fist crept over her shoulder.

With his other hand, the man must have grasped the back of the woman's filthy dress and pulled, for she shuffled backward two or three sliding steps. A face peered from around her shoulder, and a bony body followed.

The man was barefoot; the gaping waist of his patched and baggy pants was held aloft by a single suspender of frayed twine angling across his chest. The top half of a faded and filthy union suit served for a shirt, and it had been attached to the man so long that kinky hair in variegated shades of black, gray, and white sprouted through from his chest and belly.

"Who is it? What's he want?" he asked the woman.

"He's asking about Harlow Mackelprang."

"Who?"

"Harlow Mackelprang. Go back in the house." She shouldered him out of the way and again filled the doorway.

"Don't pay him no mind. He ain't right in the head. Something up there in them mines has made him touched," she said as the awareness in her eyes started to dim.

"What about Harlow Mackelprang?" I asked.

Her eyes flashed back to reality and she asked, "What about Harlow Mackelprang?"

"I'm told you cared for him after his mother died."

"I suppose I did. Had so many brats underfoot back then, I can't recall anything in particular about that one. All my own is either dead and buried or grown and gone now. Had a passel of kids and there ain't a one of 'em left around here to care for me in my old age. And I'll need it, what with him being the way he is," she said, inclining her head toward the man standing unseen just beyond the door frame. "That's the thanks you get, I guess."

"So you don't remember anything in particular about him?"

"Naw. Just another brat. They all had their mouths open all the time, either hungry or hollerin'. What you say he's gone and done?"

"He's standing trial for murder in Los Santos. You mean you haven't heard about the outlaw and gunman Harlow Mackelprang?"

"Not much news from down there gets up this high."

The woman shuddered and sidestepped as the man bumped her aside and again showed his face.

"What you want with us? We ain't got nothing to do with it." He waved the gun menacingly. "Get on out of here."

Sensing nothing of value would result from continuing the interview, I picked my way through the refuse between the house and what passed for the street. I hastened my steps considerably, increasing to a dead run, in fact, when the old pistol discharged with a roar and its projectile shattered several stacked boards a mere three feet from my own feet.

Contemplating the life of Harlow Mackelprang during the train ride back to Los Santos, I realized there was nothing of his early years that would help sell newspapers or dime novels. I determined to concentrate my efforts on his criminal activities, fleshing out my scant knowledge of events with further interviews with sources yet to be determined.

Here is what I had learned at the time, and how I learned it.

Harlow Mackelprang's depredations had commenced some six months prior to my arrival in Los Santos. According to the back issues of the newspaper that I studied, as well as information provided by Mr. Ford, the newspaper's editor and owner (and only member of the staff, save me), the crime spree commenced here in Los Santos.

It seems Harlow Mackelprang had been drinking to excess. He visited Althea, the local prostitute, who shunned his attentions and was beaten for her trouble. He then retired to the saloon, where he played cards poorly. An argument with another gambler led Harlow Mackelprang to draw his pistol without warning and shoot the other man, who was seriously wounded but not killed.

He then shot up the saloon, stole a horse from the local livery stable and wagon yard, set the barn afire either as a distraction or from pure recalcitrance, then raced out of town.

While the men of the town extinguished the blaze, the newly minted desperado used up his stolen horse almost immediately by pushing too hard, and stopped for a replacement at an outlying farm.

There, he relieved the family of a store of supplies and a less-than-suitable mount, shot and killed the farmer, and again rode away. By the time the posse arrived, his lead was too great, and so Harlow Mackelprang was lost in the hostile expanse of the desert.

Nothing more was heard of him for a few months. Then someone robbed a stagecoach, killing the driver and shotgun rider in the process. That, it seems, was Harlow Mackelprang's debut with the Catlin gang, a band of thieves and rowdies who had plundered the region hereabouts for years, all the time eluding capture and consequences. But Catlin soon dropped from the scene, and over time the outfit became Harlow Mackelprang's gang.

I asked about all this during an interview with the outlaw, and he verified all the essential details.

You see, lengthy—and not always congenial—discussions with my employer, stretching over the weeks of Harlow Mackelprang's confinement in the Los Santos lockup, had earned me the right to interview the gunman during his last night on earth.

Such a thing, Mr. Ford told me, was highly irregular at that time and in that place, the general belief being that the doomed man was entitled to, if not peace and quiet, at least protection from the badgering of the press.

But my publisher relented and said he would allow it if the marshal would.

I did not consult the marshal, inferring from previous dealings with the man what his answer would likely be. Rather, I waited at the newspaper office—which is just across the street from the jailhouse—until I saw him leave and head for the café for a late supper, knowing a visit to the saloon would likely follow.

Once he was out of the picture, I hoped I would be able to convince Charlie, the deputy, to let me interview the prisoner. But knowing there would likely be some activity at the jail through the evening, I settled in to keep an eye on the place until things quieted down.

Not long after the marshal left, Henker, that professional hangman who came in on the train the other day, showed up. I had sought an interview with him on several occasions since his arrival, only to be denied. He claimed to never submit to interviews, but invited me to buy him a drink. I declined, as I make it a practice not to ply my subjects with drink or any other incentive. Besides, he appeared to have had plenty to drink already.

A glance at the clock, when Henker departed the jail, showed he had spent less than a quarter of an hour there.

The next visitor surprised me. Decked out in a violet gown with matching hat and parasol, despite the absence of sunshine to require their use, Althea glided quickly but gracefully up the sidewalk and into the jail.

Althea, whose work as a prostitute requires the men of the town to ignore her—at least in public—

and the women in town to ignore her to the point of denying her very existence, seldom ventures out. That, and knowing something of her history with Harlow Mackelprang, made me curious as to her presence there.

I made a note to ask Charlie about that.

She stayed less than ten minutes, then stormed out of there like the devil was on her tail, and cut down the alley that would provide a shortcut to her house.

Sometime later, the preacher strode purposefully up the street, Bible in hand, and opened the jailhouse door and entered, seemingly without breaking his lengthy stride.

Although not a regular attender of church services, I am nonetheless all too well acquainted with the preacher. As I said before, Mr. Ford has assigned me myriad duties at the newspaper, one of which is dealing with the church. That was one of the first tasks he assigned me upon my taking up my position here. His glee in doing so should have served as fair warning, but I had no idea what I was getting into.

To put it mildly, our local man of God confuses his own role with that of his employer.

Unquestioning obedience is what he expects of the town and all its people, whether they are members of his congregation or not. He campaigns relentlessly to close the saloon and to forbid the sale of the devil's brew in Los Santos (an issue my employer takes personally, which is part of the reason he was glad to be relieved of direct dealings with the man).

With equal zeal, he lobbies the marshal to force Althea's removal from the town.

And he harangues me, upon the release of each and every issue of the newspaper, concerning our coverage of "unpleasant events" and the downplay, or total disregard, of his submissions of church news, gospel thoughts, and morality sermons.

His presence is imposing, and I admit to being intimidated by his first few visits. Mr. Ford merely laughed and told me to play along with the man as much as possible while in his presence, then forget everything he said and ignore his demands once he was gone.

Seeing the preacher enter the jail was not unexpected. The length of time he spent there certainly was. I could not imagine Harlow Mackelprang showing any interest in what he had to say.

Come to think of it, I could not imagine the preacher showing any interest in Harlow Mackelprang beyond telling the gunman, in no uncertain terms, that he was a sinner, deserved his fate, and was doomed to burn in hell for eternity as he was beyond hope or redemption.

I would inquire of Charlie about this curiosity as well, I thought, as I locked up the newspaper office and crossed the street to wheedle an audience with Harlow Mackelprang. Charlie seemed lost in thought as I entered, his chair being propped against the wall, hands laced behind his head, and feet propped on the desk.

"Evening, Broussard. What's up?" he asked once his eyes focused and recognition filled them.

"Just what I intended to ask you, Charlie. Big day tomorrow. Thought I'd check in and see how preparations are coming along and get a report on how Harlow Mackelprang is faring on this, his last night on earth. Anything that might be of interest to our readers, you know."

"Can't imagine what that might be. Nothing unusual going on here."

"You never know what might be newsworthy. How about if you just give me a rundown of the evening's events?"

"Well, let me see. I went over to the café and picked up Harlow Mackelprang's supper. Steak dinner, it was. Waste of good food, you ask me. Then Marshal sent me home to have my supper; said I'd be on duty here all night."

"All night? That is not often the case, is it?"

"Nah. You know that. Most times, even when we got someone locked up, we just bolt the big door and go on home."

"Is the marshal expecting trouble tonight?" I said.

"Nah, he says not. Just not wanting to take any chances."

Charlie screwed up his forehead and pursed his lips in thought, assembling an account of the evening's events.

"Let's see," he said while cogitating. "Marshal said that while I was gone that old man who's been hanging around the saloon the last few days with them two Mexicans came by and slipped Harlow Mackelprang a flask of whiskey."

"And he allowed that?"

"Surprised me too. But Marshal said it couldn't do no harm and might keep that sniveling coward from causing a scene when we string him up."

"Makes sense, I guess. Anything else?"

"Hangman came by. Strange fellow, that. He looked Harlow Mackelprang over good, said knowing his exact size and weight was important to being able to swing him properly. Hell, you ask me, I wouldn't mind seeing him strangle slowlike and painful. Anyway, the preacher came by later on."

"That's to be expected, I suppose, given the situation. Anything unusual happen with that?"

"Nah. He just went on back there and harangued Harlow Mackelprang is all."

"It seemed he was here for quite a while. Any reason for that?"

"Not that I know of. I didn't pay much attention. I did hear that fat con man we got locked up back there pitch in now and again. It was sort of like him and the preacher were ganging up on Harlow Mackelprang, or maybe going at each other. I dunno."

"Anything else, Charlie?"

"Nah, that's about it."

"Oh . . . You know, I could have sworn I saw Althea come in here after that hangman left, and then leave a few minutes later all in a huff."

"Hmmm. Saw that too, did you? She showed up all right, wanting to see Harlow Mackelprang, and I let her do it."

"What did they talk about?"

"No idea. She asked me to stay away. Wanted as much privacy as possible. When she left, I looked in on Harlow Mackelprang and he was rolled up in a ball on the floor, moaning and holding on to his privates. I didn't ask him what happened. I figured he deserved it, whatever it was. Anything Althea might've done to him wouldn't be enough."

"Thanks, Charlie. Say, you suppose I could talk to him?"

"I don't know. I guess that'd be up to the marshal."

"He isn't here. You are. Besides, what could it hurt? It ain't like he's got anything else to do."

"I reckon that's true enough. You go on back there and ask Harlow Mackelprang. If he's got no objection, I guess I don't either."

"Thanks, Charlie. I will repay the favor."

That is how I came to be the only reporter on earth to interview Harlow Mackelprang on his last night alive.

And if I cannot figure out how to write the lead to this once-in-a-lifetime story, it will all be for naught.

But as I said before, we started out the interview confirming all the whos, whats, whens, wheres, whys, and hows of his early criminal activities and his flight from Los Santos into the desert to join the Catlin gang.

"So, how did it happen that you took over leadership of the gang from Catlin?" I asked during the course of our wide-ranging late-night interview.

"I killed him. What the hell you think?"

"And the other members of the group accepted that?"

"Some of them wasn't too happy about it. I told them if they didn't like it they'd get the same. Most of them snuck off.

"Only Old Man McNulty and two Mexicans, names of Benito and Mariano, stuck with me. They's all so useless I might as well been on my own. I probably wouldn't be in the fix I'm in if it weren't for them fools.

"But it's good to have an extra gun or two sometimes, even if they can't shoot straight."

Harlow Mackelprang made it clear—for the record—that many of the misdeeds attributed to the gang were solo performances.

"That last thing I done, that deal over in Madera?"

"Yes, I know of that. You killed a traveler and the innkeeper and raped his wife, as I recall."

"Yep. That was me. Just me alone. Harlow Mackelprang don't need no help to get his name in the newspaper."

"Is that why you did it, for the publicity?"

"Hell, no, that ain't why I done it. That man who owns that rat hole should not never have messed with me. Knocked me on the head and locked me in a shed. He needed to be learned a lesson."

"But he's dead. What could he possibly have learned?"

Harlow Mackelprang laughed. "Learned quite a bit before he died, you ask me. Like how much Harlow Mackelprang enjoys taking his pleasure with a lady."

"His wife, you mean?"

"Yep. I made him watch. Then I made that ungrateful woman watch her old man die."

"What about the other man, the guest?"

"Him? He was just in the way, more or less."

"Some have asked why you didn't burn the place down."

"They wonder about that, do they? Well, ain't no reason really. Just didn't feel like it."

"But you are known for setting fires."

"I do like a nice warm fire," he said with a grin I can only describe as wicked. "First big one I set was right here in Los Santos, at the stable. That tied up folks long enough for me to get out of here.

"Set fire to a bank once, over in Robbinsville. Them folks didn't want to be robbed and gave me all kinds of trouble, so I tied 'em up and scattered around some lamp oil and dropped a match. Hear they got rescued, though. That's a shame.

"Burned up a train once, just for the hell of it. It was just sitting on a siding empty, so I figured the railroad didn't want it." Another laugh. "It weren't much use to them after I got done with it, that's for sure.

"Another time I set fire to this hacienda out southwest of here a couple, three days' ride. Mexican woman there didn't want to give me no food when I was out of supplies, or a fresh horse.

"Shot her cook dead and winged an old man who tends the barn animals before she changed her mind. Would have kept killing everyone until I got to her if she hadn't of changed her mind. But that place was all made of mud bricks, so it didn't burn too good. It got her attention, though, you bet.

"Got the attention of her old man and his vaqueros when they got home too, I bet."

"You have also stolen livestock, I am told. Is that true?"

"Sometimes. Mostly just an old cow or a yearling steer for meat, you know. Man can't be blamed for that. Time or two we took cattle to sell.

"Stole a whole herd of sheep once. Drove them stupid animals clean down into Mexico and sold them. Them that was left, that is. Lots of them died on the way. Hell, we ain't no sheepherders. How was we to know we was pushing them too hard?

"Stole lots of horses. Can't even keep track of how many. But a man's got to ride, you know. Besides, this way of getting away I learned from Catlin sure used up horses."

"Will you explain it for our readers?" I said.

"Sure. It ain't no secret. Every lawman for a hundred miles figured it out long ago. But that don't mean there was anything they could do about it.

"Alls it is, see, is that when you do a job—a big job, with the gang—you take along a bunch of extra saddle horses on the lead. Then, when the ones you're riding get tired, you just climb onto a fresh one and whack the others on the ass and scare 'em off.

"That way, see, the trail keeps splitting apart and the trackers—most of who couldn't find their ass with both hands—have to follow up every branch. Gives you lots of extra time to get away.

"After a while, they don't know or don't care anymore which trail is which and you're so far out in the desert, they have to turn back on account of they don't know where to find water."

"But you did?"

"Sure. We packed these big skins full. Enough to keep the horses going, barely. And Catlin had men what knew that desert upside down. This one greaser, Benito? He's as dumb as a stick of stove wood. Can't talk, and simpleminded to boot. But that Mexican can smell water a day away, I swear. He could turn up seeps where there weren't no sign of mud, let alone water."

"How about your hideout? Is it true that there's a place out there no one can find?"

"Hell, no, that ain't true. Indians found it long ago. I found it, didn't I? That's how I joined up with Catlin in the first place."

"How did you find it?"

"Don't rightly remember. I was pretty bad off just then. But there I was."

"Where is the place?"

"Oh, it's out there. Anyone could find it if they looked. Thing is, see, it's a long way from water.

Longer than you can ride if you don't pack water, and that's why no one hardly ever gets there.

"If they do, the layout of the place keeps 'em from getting in if you don't want 'em to. There's a few lawmen and bounty hunters and soldiers whose bones is laying out there on account of they found it. But it's in kind of a low spot, see, a little shallow canyon. It ain't too deep, maybe thirty, forty feet, but them walls is solid rock and straight up.

"Ain't but one way in or out, and that's through a narrow little gap that's barely a horse wide in spots. The way it cuts into the hill, you can't see it much 'less you know where to look. Once in that gap, you're an easy target. One man with a gun can keep out an army."

"What's it like out there?" I asked.

"Oh, it ain't much. Just a little meadow or pasture, like. I think that's what the name they call it in Mexican means—*el prado*. Up at one end there's a spring that flows enough to water the grass and provide drinking water for a pretty good horse herd and a dozen or so people.

"There's a couple shacks someone built sometime. Just sticks daubed up with mud. That, and a few ramadas to shade up under. Ain't much wood around. Few spindly cottonwoods around the spring, so you don't build no fires except to cook."

"So what's to become of *el prado* now that Harlow Mackelprang's gang is defunct?"

"Oh, someone'll use it. They's been folks hiding out there for hundreds of years, maybe more. Hell, there's even rusty old pieces of Spanish armor still laying around out there. Maybe the Indians will take the place back.

"Most likely, Mariano and them will drift back out there, maybe some other of Catlin's men too. If not them, somebody else."

We went over again some of Harlow Mackelprang's crimes, just to assure that I had the facts straight—from his perspective. Most of them, of course, were familiar to me.

While some outlaws go to great lengths to avoid association with their crimes, Harlow Mackelprang took every opportunity for publicity, announcing his name to victims and witnesses alike. I wondered why.

"How long you been in these parts, Broussard?"

"More than two years. Not quite three."

"So you came to Los Santos not long after I left town."

"That is correct. There was still much speculation at the time about your involvement in the stage-coach robbery over in the Thunder Mountains, not far from Trueno."

"That was me all right. That was my first job with Catlin's outfit. But I didn't need their help. Pulled that one off all by myself before they even knew it happened. But we been over that already."

"True. We were merely establishing the time of my arrival in Los Santos."

"Yeah?"

"You were going to tell me why you have sought publicity for your crimes."

"Oh, yeah. Well, you know, I grew up here most of my life. Didn't have a ma. Old man's a drunk. So folks here treated me like I was nothing. Less than nothing, in fact. Well, they can see I'm something now. Ain't none of them ever gonna forget Harlow Mackelprang came to town."

"Is that important to you?"

"Hell, yes! All these people who can't wait to see me hung ain't gonna amount to nothing in this world. They think they're so damn important, but you just wait. Once their bones are in the dirt, nobody will even remember they were alive. At least when Harlow Mackelprang did something crooked, he did it up big. Not like them petty crooks."

"What do you mean?"

"You mean you ain't seen it? What kind of newsman are you, can't see what's right under your nose?"

"I guess you will have to tell me about it."

"Sure I will. Start right on the other side of that wall there. Marshal gets paid off by Althea every month. The saloon too, I think to keep his nose out of their crooked card games. Besides paying him off, they stand him to free drinks any time he's thirsty. And just ask Costello or Lila over to the café when he last paid for a meal there."

"Small potatoes, don't you think?"

"Yeah, that's what I said in the first place. It's small-time stuff."

"Who else?"

"Ask that sissy Tueller at the bank for a look at his books. He cheated me once, and I know I ain't the only one. And he learned it from his uncle, old man Fargo.

"There's more. Them over at the mercantile cheat everybody that comes in. Just a little bit, but it adds up. I've seen it.

"Know where Costello gets all that beef for the café? Well, I do, 'cause he got some of it from me. And they put all manner of stuff that ain't liquor in the drinks at the saloon, besides cheatin' at cards.

"Aah, what's the use? They all steal from each other and nobody cares, long as they can smile and pretend it ain't happening. But let old Harlow Mackelprang come along and it's a different deal."

He's right, of course, about the petty graft and cheating. While I was not aware of some of what he related, much of it is common knowledge.

Even my own newspaper is not entirely innocent, shaving a few agate lines from advertisements here and there to save space, with the reduction in size neither acknowledged nor accompanied by a reduction in price.

But such insignificant wrongdoing is not the thing upon which journalistic careers are built. "Uncovering" such malfeasance in Los Santos would be met with a resounding yawn, if such reporting were even allowed to appear on the pages of the newspaper, which, I can assure you, it would not.

No, the exploits of Harlow Mackelprang are more newsworthy and more interesting. And his story is the horse I will ride to fame and fortune.

If I can just figure out the damn lead.

SWEENEY

Harlow Mackelprang's last supper offered a welcome, if brief, respite from the rank odors normally present in this confining chamber.

Even now, I can imagine the sharp smell of sauerkraut with subtler undertones of beef and gravy. Sadly, it is only imagination, as the persistence of the aroma from a mere plate of food is no match for the years of accumulated stink and collected stench from unwashed men and their bodily functions with which I share this cell.

From a strictly culinary standpoint, his repast was a cruel reminder that biscuits and beans, served alternately with beans and biscuits, all washed down with foul and tepid water, comprise the sum total of the fare available to the average inmate in the Los Santos jail.

Harlow Mackelprang, of course, is not the average inmate. Even now, the gunman is on his way to the gallows to pay the ultimate price for his crimes. Thus, the young outlaw was allowed the courtesy of choosing the *carte du jour* for his final meal.

It is a shame in a way. The manner in which he bolted it down made it obvious that he lacked appreciation for the comestibles. And as lean as he is, it is likewise obvious that food is mere sustenance to him, rather than an agreeable indulgence. Much better to offer such fare to one such as I, who truly admires a well-cooked meal and whose corpulence corroborates the fact.

On the other hand, if the only escape from routine rations is the final meal prior to execution, beans and biscuits twice a day every day is entirely satisfactory. After four days, I suspect I have grown accustomed to the diet. I truly hope, however, that I am released from this cell before I begin to actually enjoy it.

I find myself, by the way, in the embarrassing condition of incarceration through no fault of my own. An unfortunate dispute over the terms of a business arrangement led to my internment. I assure you, however, that I will be cleared of wrongdoing and released immediately upon the opportunity to stand before the circuit judge and relate the circumstances of the disagreement.

The events leading to my present difficulties were set in motion upon my arrival in Los Santos a week ago Tuesday. After taking up lodgings in what passes for a hotel in this burg, I ordered my sample cases and trunk fetched from the railroad station, enjoyed a passable late breakfast at the café, then paid a visit to the local newspaper to place an order with the editor, Mr. Ford, for a display ad announcing my presence in the town and outlining, briefly, the opportunities my presence here provides.

Then I make it a practice to visit one or more of the

banks in town and seek to interview the manager. This last has proved a useful part of my routine upon arriving in fresh territory, as I am often successful in ferreting out the identities of individuals with the assets and inclination to qualify as investors—investments being my line.

Among my offerings at present are a number of mineral-exploration-and-extraction firms, a few select ventures incorporated for the purpose of acquiring land for a variety of commercial purposes, including livestock grazing and the development of residential communities, some irrigation and canal enterprises, and a private railroad company currently surveying branch lines by which to spread prosperity from established main lines to outlying communities.

The security and protection available through life insurance policies are also among my portfolio of offerings.

From time to time, when other avenues aren't producing, I have been known to promote patent medicines for a firm in the East.

And always and at every opportunity, I will show a beautifully made family Bible with gilt-edged pages and color plates illustrating pivotal scenes and events from the text. Although not particularly profitable, I consider Bible sales of utmost importance and view the reduced compensation that results as my personal contribution to the betterment of mankind and the civilization of the Western country.

It is one such Bible from my stock that the marshal has kindly allowed me to keep in my cell that has proved the only barrier between myself and insanity during my confinement here.

The holy tome has been my constant companion

for years. The many idle hours I have spent aboard trains, in hotel rooms, in stagecoaches, and at camp-sites scattered far and wide across the land have resulted in my more-than-passing familiarity with the Good Book. I have perused its pages numerous times, and am conversant with its major themes as well as many of the subtleties and mysteries found among its pages.

But I have diverged from the intended path of my narrative.

As I stated earlier, once settled in at the hotel, I paid a visit to the local bank and requested an interview with the manager.

Frankly, he was less than helpful, seeming distracted throughout our conversation. When I offered to call at a more convenient time, as he seemed preoccupied just then, the young man—Tueller, by name—said that there wouldn't likely be a better time, at least not for another week or so. Upon my further inquiries, he saw in me the opportunity to unburden himself to a sympathetic ear.

"These are trying times, Mr. Sweeney," he said. "I am at present burdened with the training of a new clerk—the woman you just met—the lingering strain of testifying at a murder trial, the anxiety of witnessing the execution of the criminal five days from now, and the shock of recently watching the cold-blooded killing of a dear friend and associate within these very walls."

For some time, he regaled me with the details. As he concluded, I offered my sympathy.

"A difficult time indeed. Is there some aid or assistance I might offer, Mr. Tueller?"

"Thank you, but I think not. Perhaps after the

hanging I will be able to put all this behind me and get back to a more routine existence."

"I certainly hope so. I certainly hope so," I said. "I shall not trouble you with the details in these circumstances, Mr. Tueller, but allow me to say that I am at present authorized to offer a particularly prime opportunity for a discerning individual or individuals with the foresight—and the means—to invest in this potential bonanza."

"I am not at liberty to divulge such information as it relates to the bank's customers. Surely you are aware of that, Sweeney."

"Certainly. Of course. I am not asking you to divulge any confidences, nor would I accept such information if offered.

"However, as the manager of the bank, you are no doubt aware of men of your acquaintance who wish to better their financial position. Such information is usually the subject of discussion in public houses and on the streets, but I have found that gentlemen in your position are more discerning and can save me the time it takes to distill such gossip, if you will, into useful leads."

"I see. I suppose there is no harm in providing the names of local men whose prosperity is common knowledge. And I can name a few others whom I have heard—again, from public discussions and not from private conversations related to my position here or their deposits or dealings with the bank—have a desire to hasten their accumulation of capital."

"Such information would be most appreciated, I assure you, Mr. Tueller. As a token of my appreciation, please accept this handsome copy of the Holy Bible. As you see, it is a beautifully gilded edition, enhanced copiously with colored works of art. It is as well the family-tree version with space provided to record your genealogy and the birth and baptismal dates of your children as well as other notable occasions. I am sure you will find it a useful and valuable addition to your home and family."

"A generous offer, Sweeney, but one I must refuse. Not that I question its propriety. It is only that I have neither a family nor an affinity for religion."

"Most unfortunate, Mr. Tueller. Perhaps a little browsing in your spare moments will bring about a change of heart—at least so far as developing an appreciation for its message."

"I think not. I am not totally unfamiliar with its contents. It is just that they bring more confusion than comfort. And just now, I need comfort more than confusion."

"As you wish. Perhaps I can still be of assistance. Upon my return to the hotel I shall send a messenger over with a twelve-ounce bottle of Doctor Wolff's Formula. It is an exclusive preparation of medicinal herbs and other beneficial ingredients used to the benefit of many thousands on the European continent for many years. It will, I assure you, provide sufficient comfort to allow you to relax, even as it builds strength in the internal organs and bolsters your stamina both physically and emotionally."

Tueller accepted that offer, if somewhat skeptically, then proceeded to relate the details of the financial histories and circumstances of a goodly number of his neighbors and customers. There were many prospects to choose from.

I chose badly.

I shall not belabor the details, all of which will be

revealed in court. Briefly, from the list of prospects assembled, I opted to approach a gentleman named Fargo who had invested significant sums in a broad region of the territory centered on the community of Las Santos. Fargo is, in fact, the principal owner and retired manager of the local bank and, as I was informed later, Tueller's uncle.

Upon gaining an audience with the financier, I presented him with a proposal to invest heavily in the Alta Paso Short Line Railway Company, an endeavor focused on laying track over a rugged mountain pass to connect a prosperous mining district with the main line of a major railroad.

Fargo was hesitant at first, being unfamiliar with the distant territory, as the project is located several hundred miles from Los Santos. My representations eventually proved persuasive, however, and I was pleased to leave the meeting with a sizable check in hand, a receipt for which was duly provided along with a provisional stock certificate issued pending the recording of the investment in Alta Paso's books and issuance of officially certified stock documents.

Imagine my chagrin when the following morning the marshal knocked upon my hotel room door and asked that I accompany him to his office. Upon arrival there, I was confronted by Fargo, who accused me of being a liar, a cheat, and a swindler engaged in a confidence game.

According to Fargo's version of events, immediately following our transaction he contacted by telegraph an acquaintance of his who serves on the board of the main-line railroad company through which the Alta Paso Short Line will establish a physical connection to the wider rail network.

This board member denied knowledge of any such arrangement or even the existence of the firm I represent, and pronounced the entire thing a fraud.

According to this gentleman's representations to Mr. Fargo, numerous investigations had been made into just such a rail line, but all had concluded that the mountains are so steep and rugged that the venture is not economically feasible.

Fargo's position in the community being what it is, the marshal accepted his accusations and insinuations as sufficient cause for my arrest, and would not even allow explanation on my part. I was seized on the spot and have been held in this jail cell subsequently, awaiting the arrival of the circuit judge.

Even the judge, contacted by wire, approved of my incarceration and denied me bail. Obviously, His Honor is biased toward, if not in the pocket of, my accuser. Nevertheless, I shall welcome my appearance before him and am confident of my subsequent release. I will, as a sign of good faith, offer to return the aforementioned check to Mr. Fargo and shall release him from his contractual obligations and let bygones be bygones. It is not my intention, nor has it ever been my method, to encourage prospects to invest in ventures in which they are not confident, nor to maintain an investment position with which they are not entirely comfortable. Within, of course, the bounds of contract law.

In hindsight, perhaps I should have proposed that Fargo invest in an irrigation project in the Arapaho River Valley in which I have an interest. Or, given his experience with the vagaries related to the location and extraction of deposits of valuable minerals, I might have presented him with one or even several of the hopeful mining prospects I represent. The risks associated with railroading, it seems, are a bit rich for his taste, resulting in this instance in a case of cold feet.

But be that as it may, I have no alternative at present to biding my time. With the permanent absence of Harlow Mackelprang pending, it will be a lonely existence.

We have not conversed a great deal, he and I, over the hours and days we have spent together. Not that there hasn't been talk, you understand—on the contrary, Harlow Mackelprang has talked a good deal. But there has been little in the way of *conversation*.

Asking Harlow Mackelprang a question, I have learned, is tantamount to releasing a rabbit before a pack of hounds. Once the question is asked, he cannot be stopped or redirected in his answers and he pursues the topic relentlessly.

Consequently, he has told me much about his criminal activities.

He does not deny responsibility. In fact, he relishes the notoriety that has resulted from his misdeeds. He takes a certain perverse pride in being known and feared across the territory, and views it as a significant accomplishment.

He feels no guilt for the harm he has done, nor does he see his acts as criminal or even wrong. He claims the people of Los Santos—and all humankind, in fact—deserve whatever he has given them, and that his crimes are but small repayment for the evils perpetrated against him.

And so I am of the firm opinion that Harlow Mackelprang views himself as the innocent in all this, and is not troubled in the least by guilt or remorse.

Twisted as it may seem to some, he will meet his Maker—in whom he most decidedly does not believe—with a clear conscience. He has related to me that since killing his first man, his sleep has not been troubled in the least, nor have additional deaths at his hand changed that fact.

A visitor, a compatriot of his, I believe, called Mariano, scoffed at my suggestion that Harlow Mackelprang, who was napping at the time, slept the sleep of the innocent.

But such is, in fact, the case.

While the man is patently *not* innocent in the eyes of the law, and is decidedly guilty in the eyes of his fellow citizens, and is certainly a mortal sinner of the worst degree in the eyes of God, Harlow Mackelprang, in his own mind, has done no wrong.

That, at least, is my assessment of the situation. And despite my presence in this cell suggesting contrariwise, I am adept at judging human character and motivations, and must continuously cultivate these abilities in order to earn my daily bread.

Mariano, whom I mentioned earlier, was, to my knowledge, the only visitor to these quarters prior to last evening. Since then, it has been a virtual parade of characters the likes of which one finds richly represented in the pages of the New Testament.

He has been visited, at various times, by men bearing gifts, by the lame, by a Pharisee, by a scribe, by the executioner, even by a woman taken in adultery.

And now, Harlow Mackelprang has been taken out by the authorities to be killed.

Please do not misinterpret the foregoing statement.

It would be preposterous, of course, to draw comparisons between this man and Jesus Christ, the hero of the New Testament being truly innocent while Harlow Mackelprang is innocent only in his own twisted mind.

Nevertheless, in cases where a life is to be taken, one cannot help but recall Christ's admonition, "He that is without sin among you, let him cast the first stone."

Every one of Harlow Mackelprang's visitors came here to cast stones, and none offered so much as a kind word to comfort him while in prison, as the Master commands.

The marshal never passed up an opportunity to remind the prisoner of his criminal behavior and the need to repay society for violating the law of the land. Again and again he made the case.

It is as if, somehow, that endless repetition serves to convince the marshal that his own role in these events is justified.

Even so simple an act as the performance of his duty in delivering a meal to the condemned occasioned ire and resentment on the part of the young deputy. He could not resist belittling the imprisoned and begrudging him his last supper.

A visit from the condemned's erstwhile companion, called McNulty by his host, served to upset rather than calm Harlow Mackelprang. I sensed that this was, in fact, the visitor's motive all along—more so than the delivery of a flask of whiskey. The man seemed to bait the bandit leader, teasing him in subtle ways that his victim did not discern.

The hangman came by to take Harlow Mackelprang's measurements and to educate the man about the particulars of a hanging. He did so, it seems, only to facilitate his performance of the unpleasant task, and not to contribute to the condemned's ease with the situation. In fact, he made no bones about the fact that the gunman's death was of little or no consequence; merely another job of work.

And Althea. The lovely Althea, whose acquaintance I would enjoy making in more congenial circumstances (and may yet), arrived here solely to extract some measure of revenge. In some sense, her cause was just. But how much greater would her reward have been had she offered forgiveness rather than reprisal.

And the preacher.

While I sat as silent witness to the other visitors this night, I could not hold my tongue in the presence of that self-righteous excuse for a man of God.

To hear him tell it, one would be led to believe that the Holy Bible ended with the Book of Malachi. He regaled Harlow Mackelprang with "thou shalt nots" and blood and revenge from the Old Testament as if the grace and mercy and forgiveness of Our Savior had no place in our earthly travail.

Not that it made much difference to Harlow Mackelprang, he being devoid of any religious inclinations.

Be that as it may, it is my belief that one of the Lord's messengers ought to lend comfort to a sinner in Harlow Mackelprang's situation, rather than torment the poor soul with more affliction.

The reporter who visited cared little about recording the views of Harlow Mackelprang for posterity. His motive was grasping greed and lowly pride, with the gunman nothing more than a tool. The interview offered the possibility for the hopeful scribe to aggrandize himself at the expense of the condemned's unfortunate circumstances and reap filthy lucre for a reward.

Ah, but who am I to pass judgment? I am in no better position to cast a stone than any other man. I sometimes fear, in moments of deep contemplation, that my means of livelihood would not bear close scrutiny.

Then again, whose would?

It is with the best of intentions that I represent the enterprises in my portfolio.

After all, who am I to say that the Alta Paso Short Line Railway will not be built?

Who is to say the Arapaho Valley irrigation project will not hold water?

How can one know in advance if a mining claim will or will not pan out?

If the promoters say they intend to develop a project, I take them at their word. There is risk, of course. Every investment inherently carries a certain amount of risk, and I always, always, include in my sales presentations a reminder of that fact (even though I may tend to downplay that aspect of the transaction).

And when it comes right down to it, an investor who risks money he cannot afford to lose is, at best, imprudent and, more likely, a fool. My motives are likewise with life insurance, Doctor Wolff's preparation, or even the Good Book itself.

My responsibility is only on making such available; it is the duty of the buyer to determine the wisdom of the investment or expenditure.

I am sure the judge, if well read on the statutes, will be cognizant of these facts—facts according to law, if not ethics—and will readily dismiss the complaint against me. The allegations will be expunged, my record with the legal system cleared, and my good name restored.

Fraud is, after all, such an ugly, ugly word.

As for now, I wait.

And I wait alone, for the time being. I must say that after the parade of visitors throughout the evening and into the night, the solitude is not altogether unwelcome. In fact, in more salubrious circumstances and with better accommodations, I might find privacy of this degree desirable. In this jail cell, however, it is discomfiting.

Once Harlow Mackelprang was led away, a silence descended upon this place like a pall.

No one, of course, occupies a cell here now save myself. No marshal or deputy stirs in the outer office. No footsteps nor hoofbeats nor the rattle of trace chains filter in through the window.

The only sound is the distant hum created by the crowd—every man, woman, and child from Los Santos and for miles around, I suspect—that has gathered to witness the demise of Harlow Mackelprang.

Why they choose to do so escapes me. Turning death into a celebratory festival is a savage and brutal practice, and one we must abandon if we are to become a truly civilized society.

Alas, it is not to be.

So I wish they would hang Harlow Mackelprang and get it over with so life can return to some semblance of normalcy. Starting, I should hope, with this morning's ration of biscuits and beans. Or is it beans and biscuits this time?

I shall be glad to see it in either case.

TUELLER

Harlow Mackelprang's last supper will soon be a malodorous mess in the seat of his trousers.

Such nasty facts of life (or should I say death?) are not often associated with the genteel life of a banker. But being raised the son of an undertaker, I have personal knowledge of such things. Oftentimes at death, and virtually always in cases of sudden or violent death, bladder and bowel involuntarily vacate.

I do not know how many in the crowd here this morning to witness the hanging of Harlow Mackelprang are aware of this curious fact. But I know that many will become aware once his neck is stretched.

And yet the unfortunate aspect of this unpleasantness is that the man himself will not be aware of it. The stink will not haunt him, as the odor of blood haunts me. His skin will not be irritated by the warmth and wetness, the way mine quivers still at the memory of trickling gore. He will not stand elbow-deep in wash water, attempting to grind away with soap and scrub board the stains he leaves on his own clothing, as I have attempted to remove the crimson stains his deed left on mine.

And no longer will his spirit (if he has one) and mind be troubled (if ever they were) as mine are by the image of a human body being blown apart before his eyes.

I have felt guilt and shame these past three weeks because I did not act to prevent the awful deed.

I attempt to justify my inaction with the belief that there was nothing I *could* have done; no action I might have taken would have altered the course of events in any significant way or changed the outcome. The marshal shares this belief, and has made every attempt to relieve my guilt.

And yet I wonder—*would* I have acted if circumstances had allowed?

I do not know.

I suppose I will never know.

And I am not altogether certain that I *want* to know.

Having been raised during the formative years of my life (*all* my life, in fact, until moving to Los Santos to manage my uncle's bank) in the peaceful, genteel city of Franklin, Pennsylvania, I was not accustomed to the "life of action" that seems prevalent among men here in the West.

As I said, my father was an undertaker with a thriving practice. I was always bookish by nature and, I see now, overindulged by my parents. The result of this upbringing was a delicate boy who became a delicate man.

Aimless and lacking direction, I languished at the university for a number of years until Mother's brother suggested that I come West to learn the banking business and take over management of his bank in Los Santos.

(An ulterior motive, no doubt, of my uncle and my parents in this gesture was the belief that exposure to the rugged ways of the frontier would serve to "toughen me up" and make a man of me.)

And so here I have lived these past fourteen years.

My journey west was, in every aspect, an eye-opening experience. Although I was able to cover the entire distance in the relative comfort and safety of the railroad, and was not required to "rough it" in stagecoaches or on horseback, the amenities certainly diminished with distance from home.

As I made my way across the continent, the main lines divided into branches, then into feeder lines to serve the larger railroads, and finally the nearly empty rails that ended (as I would later learn) in the mountains at Meeker's Mill, not far beyond my destination of Los Santos.

As the railroads probed further from civilization, so too did the trains that traveled on them—cars and trains, made up for the comfort and convenience of the passenger trade, were jettisoned, replaced with conveyances to accommodate freight and livestock. Pullman coaches dropped off, leaving only upholstered cars for passengers. Then these gave way to noisy, drafty, rattletrap cars equipped only with wooden benches.

The rest of the world, too, changed with the approach and arrival of the West.

The forests to which I was accustomed lined the rails for days, broken naturally only by a watercourse, or where the woods had been cleared for farms and villages. Further west, the skeletons of girdled trees were still evident, along with stumps in the fields and yards.

Later still, the trees diminished, then seemingly disappeared altogether, replaced by an endless rolling carpet of grass. The prairies gave way to plains; the grass grew sparse, bunched and clustered across a land broken, irregular, and uneven.

That too gave way to desolation and desert. The land and everything on it—what little was on it—were all the same monotonous hues of dusty, sunfaded browns, dry and hard as cracked leather.

The confinement of the East was gone. No more limited views or close surroundings. I had entered a world without borders or boundaries. Nothing, in any direction, could restrict one's outlook, except discomfort with the wide unknown.

The landscape's lack of restraint spilled over onto the people as well, washing away convention and social graces. The genteel first-class travelers at the beginning of my journey slowly but surely deteriorated until they too became rough, unkempt, crude; later as dull, hard, and hostile as the accommodations and the landscape.

Most of the travelers were by then men. They were unwashed, for the most part, and the stink of their bodies blended with the stench of whatever mixture of blood, mud, grease, and grime coated their outerwear in thick layers. I dared not contemplate the state of their underwear.

One night as the train clattered along, I attempted sleep—with one eye open—while a gambling game of cards carried on in the car. The players dealt the pasteboards out on a plank balanced on their knees, which was loudly upset when one jumped to his feet.

"You're cheatin' me!" he shouted, attempting to pull a pistol from his belt.

I suspect he would have drawn and fired the piece had he not been so inebriated—a crockery jug of some foul mixture having made it around the table as often as the cards.

Two other players rolled and slid sideward to distance themselves from the fumbling gunman while the third stood, revealing a knife from somewhere on his person as he rose. It was a large skinning knife, perhaps two inches deep from top of blade to bottom, and a good ten inches of length extended from the man's hand. I could see, in the instant, it was well used, as repeated sharpening had created a slight concave curve along the cutting surface.

The knife-wielder said, "Sit down, you damn fool," to the man still fumbling for his gun. "You're just too damn drunk to read the spots on the cards."

"You're a cheat!"

"Leave that gun in that leather, or I'll lay you open. I swear I will."

Obviously the drunker of the two, the one with the pistol continued his awkward attempts to extricate the revolver, which he finally did, drawing back the hammer with an ominous metallic snap and click. But before the piece could be leveled in the direction of its target, the knife blade flashed, slicing through a filthy cloth coat and shirt fabric to cut a lengthy gash across the angle of the forearm holding the pistol.

I believe to this day that I heard the tick of the blade bouncing off bone.

The injured man let loose his grip on the pistol, which dropped to the floor and hit with a clunk among the scattered cards and coin as his free hand grasped the cut arm.

"You knifed me, you sorry bastard!" he screamed in disbelief as blood welled from between his fingers and pitter-patted in crimson drops to the floor, further soiling the greasy cards.

"I told you to leave that gun alone."

"I'm bleedin', damn you!"

"You're lucky you ain't dead. If we wasn't partners I'd have let your guts out where you stand."

He again thrust the knife toward the injured man, who flinched at the motion. But he turned the knife blade sideways and wiped both sides clean of blood on the front of his victim's shirt. "Now get the hell out of my sight before I change my mind."

The bleeding man stumbled—whether faint from his injury or from lack of sobriety I cannot say—toward and beyond me to the end of the car, where he propped himself on the bench in a dark corner, still clutching his wound. In the dim fringe of the light of the lanterns hanging in the coach, the blood looked black as it seeped through his fingers and the stain spread through the coarse weave of the grimy fabric of his coat sleeve.

There are other examples I could proffer of the shock and excitement of my introduction to the frontier. Few incidents were as violent as the altercation on the train, but many events served to school me in the harsh manner in which men dealt with one another.

I was, obviously, unprepared for such means and methods. Still, I settled in at Los Santos in the relative safety of my uncle's family, and proceeded to learn the banking business. Over the course of a few years I mastered the job and managed to establish myself in a serviceable and independent bachelor household of my own.

Since managing the basics of the bank's operations, I have become expert with experience, and my uncle has barely set foot in the place for a number of years. I might add that my ability to maximize the limited financial opportunities available here has contributed to making his retirement a comfortable one. I should say as well that I have enjoyed banking and Los Santos and have made every effort to fit in, and feel I have become accepted in this wild and rough place.

But after being showered with bits and pieces of my clerk's bodily parts and fluids, and enduring the aftermath of that awful occasion, I am no longer sure if I will (or even *can*) remain here.

Living that terrible day was very trying. Reliving it as one of only two witnesses at Harlow Mackelprang's murder trial was only marginally less so.

"Mr. Tueller, what is your position at the bank?" the prosecutor asked, once the formalities of swearing in and identifying myself were out of the way.

"My office is that of vice president. My job is that of manager."

"And were you at work in the bank on the day in question?"

"Yes."

"Please recount your recollection of the events of that day as they relate to the defendant, Harlow Mackelprang."

"I was at my desk, as usual, writing correspondence and doing book work. As always, it was a quiet day. A few customers had visited earlier, but only

Calvin, the clerk, and myself were in the bank when the door burst open and a man strode in carrying a gun. A shotgun, I believe, with a short barrel."

"Did you recognize the man?"

"Certainly. It was Harlow Mackelprang. He used to live here. In Los Santos, I mean."

Harlow Mackelprang was already a fixture in the community when I arrived in Los Santos. Stories of his doings were continuously grinding through the rumor mills. It seemed that wherever trouble reared its head, he was involved (or suspected of being so). He was caught often enough to lend credence to the suspicions, but it would not surprise me if other youthful (or even adult) offenders got away with any number of transgressions that were blamed on Harlow Mackelprang as a matter of course.

Tales were told of his stealing all manner of things, from a pie cooling on a windowsill to the theft, then abuse or killing of animals. Besides thievery, he was a known bully who took advantage of anyone smaller or weaker.

He avoided confrontation with all others, they say, because of cowardice and fear. He was also branded a sneak and a Peeping Tom. I do not doubt that all of these accusations had their basis in fact, but I would not be surprised if there were exaggerations at work as well.

In any event, virtually anything that happened in Los Santos that was beyond the pale of law or common decency was entered as a debit against Harlow Mackelprang. If there were any entries in his asset column, I was never made aware of the fact. (But that may be because no one would have given him credit for any good deed he *might* have committed.)

As I recall, things took a turn for the worse so far as the criminal history of Harlow Mackelprang is concerned about three years ago.

He had reached his majority about that time and had taken up drinking in a serious way. (Not that he hadn't been a drinker prior to that time; he simply became more public about it.) One would think that the difficulties drink had created for his father (a famous lush) would have made him cognizant of the ill effects of alcohol, but such, apparently, was not the case.

As the story was told to me, a bout of drinking and gambling at the local saloon got out of hand and an altercation with another cardplayer led to gunplay, resulting in Harlow Mackelprang's wounding of the other player. He then, they say, discharged several more rounds into the glassware and fixtures of the saloon. From all accounts, thus began his career as a gunman.

In order to get away, he then appropriated a horse and tack at the livery stable and set that structure ablaze.

Later, I learned there was more. He had visited Althea, a local lady of the evening, earlier. (I am well acquainted with Althea, incidentally, on a professional level—my profession, not hers—and know that most people in Los Santos would be surprised at the balances she maintains in accounts at the bank.) For whatever reason, he had mistreated Althea terribly and she was some days recovering from his beating.

After leaving Los Santos, he robbed a struggling farm family and killed the man of the house in cold blood. (A little-known result of this crime was an unpaid debt at the bank, requiring an unfortunate foreclosure. The bank still holds the deed to that marginal property, and I doubt we will ever be able to shift it.)

As for any personal relationship or unpleasant encounters with Harlow Mackelprang, I have nothing to relate. Other than the day of the robbery and killing, I can recall only two occasions upon which he set foot in the bank.

The first occurred when he was about seventeen years old, I suppose. I accepted for deposit an amount of money (sixty-three dollars, if memory serves) he brought into the bank.

I confess that I did not, however, actually put the money on deposit. Suspecting something nefarious in the acquisition of the funds, I intended to notify the marshal, so I placed the money in one of my personal accounts for temporary safekeeping.

But in the press of business I never accomplished the task of notifying the marshal, and so the money languished there. When the incident next crossed my mind, so much time had passed that I believed the interval too great for any good to come from reporting my suspicions, so I (I am ashamed to confess) decided to let sleeping dogs lie, as they say, and the money remained in my account.

Harlow Mackelprang's deposit again came to my attention subsequent to his second visit to the bank.

It occurred more than a year later (fourteen months, to be precise) when he returned to withdraw the funds. I was not in the bank that day, being out and about in the countryside visiting farmers and stockmen who were indebted to the bank, delivering payment notices and gentle reminders. I was also, you might say, keeping an eye on the bank's investments.

So the clerk was on duty alone at the bank that day. He (his name was Waldo, this being prior to Calvin's tenure with us) could find no record of any account in the name of Harlow Mackelprang. Nor was there any notation or entry in the ledgers to record the deposit or to credit the accumulation of interest.

Harlow Mackelprang, of course, did not have one of the booklets the bank provides customers, in which we record account activity and update it for the account holder on each visit to the bank.

After enduring considerable verbal abuse, Waldo eventually convinced Harlow Mackelprang that he had no money on deposit. (Or at least Harlow Mackelprang realized the futility of his claim given his own ignorance of the ways and means of financial transactions.)

After all these years, the money is still there somewhere. But I do not recall which of my accounts holds the money and, to be honest with you, I would not be able to separate the deposit (or the interest earned and accumulated) from the personal funds with which it has mingled all these years.

That summarizes my personal knowledge of and experience with Harlow Mackelprang right up to the day, three weeks ago, that he committed robbery and homicide in my presence.

And, of course, my experience in the courtroom last week.

"Is the man who came into the bank, the one you call Harlow Mackelprang, in this courtroom today?" the prosecutor asked.

"Of course. He is sitting right there."

"Thank you. Please go on."

"Another man—he appeared to be Mexican—followed him in. The second man stopped by the door, looked around for a moment, then left."

"Is it your belief that this second man was with the defendant?"

"It is. He had a pistol in his hand. But as I said, he did not stay. He slipped away."

"Did you see where he went, Mr. Tueller?"

"I did not. Harlow Mackelprang was waving his gun around and shouting, so my attention was on him.

"He ordered me to stand up, raise my hands, and step to the side of the desk. He threw a cloth sack at Calvin and told him to put all the money in it.

"Calvin did as he was told, all the while protesting to Harlow Mackelprang that he would not get away with it. This seemed to upset him—Harlow Mackelprang, I mean—and he grew considerably more agitated with each passing moment.

"Calvin emptied the cash drawer and attempted to pass the sack back to Harlow Mackelprang, but he demanded that the safe also be emptied. Our bank does not have a vault; merely a small safe that sits on the floor behind the manager's—my—desk. Calvin added the few stacks of currency and some gold coin from the safe to the sack, then handed it to Harlow Mackelprang.

"Then Harlow Mackelprang called out—to the other man who had come in with him, I presumed—asking if the coast was clear. When the other man did not answer, he became even more upset. Visibly, almost insanely so. He kept calling for the man—Mariano was the name he used. Calvin told him once again that he wouldn't get away with this, which upset him even more.

"He started backing slowly toward the door, pointing his gun back and forth between us and calling out for his accomplice. Then Calvin said again, 'You won't get away with this,' and 'We know who you are. You are Harlow Mackelprang.'

"At this, Harlow Mackelprang shouted, 'You're damn right I am. And don't you forget it.'"

"Was that all he said?"

"Yes, sir. That is all."

"Then what happened, Mr. Tueller?"

"He shot him."

"I'm sorry Mr. Tueller. I know this is painful. But the record must be clear on this point. Who shot who?"

"Harlow Mackelprang shot Calvin."

"Do you remember how many shots were fired?"

"Just one. That's all it took to kill Calvin. It blew him to pieces. I was standing just behind him, a little to the side. The shot splattered blood and bits of him all over me."

As I related the story in court, tears streamed down my cheeks, as warm and wet as the streams of Calvin's blood had been.

Some of the townspeople in the courtroom seemed uncomfortable with my display of emotion on the stand, and I confess embarrassment. But I could not help myself. The tears came then, as they still do on occasion, unbidden and unexpected. Seeing a young man one has worked with side by side, day by day, and grown to love, get shot to pieces is not easily dealt with so soon after the fact.

I only hope that with the passage of time I will at

least be able to control my emotions, as I cannot face life if it is to be lived as these past three weeks have been.

I find myself weeping silently and am surprised by the discovery. I no longer sleep well, due to nightmares. I lose concentration at work—a regular occurrence these days—and drift into daydreams, only to be startled back to reality by visions of Calvin's blood spraying me.

Even being in the bank is almost more than I can bear, as everything there serves to remind me of the robbery and the murder.

"A most unfortunate experience, Mr. Tueller," the prosecutor said. "Can you continue?"

"Yes. Yes. I am sorry. After shooting Calvin, Harlow Mackelprang turned and ran out the door, but was upended and fell to the sidewalk. The marshal was waiting outside the door and tripped him up. Then the marshal was standing over him, with a pistol at Harlow Mackelprang's head."

"Why was the marshal there? Had an alarm been sounded?"

"The bank does not have an alarm. I did not even wonder at the time how the marshal came to be there. I was so grateful that he was there that it did not occur to me to wonder why."

"Thank you, Mr. Tueller. That will be all."

The only other witness at Harlow Mackelprang's trial was the marshal. His testimony was brief.

He told of how an old man on horseback leading another horse had ridden up in front of his office, called him out, told him—his deputy actually—that the bank was being robbed, and then had ridden away with a second man, who mounted his horse on the street in front of the bank.

It was the marshal's contention, passed on to me in private conversation, that these were Harlow Mackelprang's confederates who had, for some reason, orchestrated the betrayal of their associate.

The marshal testified that he concealed himself next to the open front door of the bank in an attempt to assess the situation inside, only to be startled by the shotgun blast. Then the marshal told, as I had, how Harlow Mackelprang ran out the door and he tripped him and placed him under arrest.

The jury required mere moments to return a guilty verdict, and the judge sentenced Harlow Mackelprang to be hanged in a week's time. From start to finish, the entire procedure took less than one hour.

An hour that I may never recover from.

And one that Harlow Mackelprang certainly never will.

Now, here I stand on the streets of Los Santos, on the very route Harlow Mackelprang will take when escorted by the marshal to the gallows just moments from now. After the hanging, I will retire to the bank and prepare for the day's opening.

One advantage of keeping banker's hours is that a hanging on an early summer's morn does not interfere with the normal course of business. Which course of business nowadays involves training a new clerk.

I have engaged a woman for the position, despite the protestations of my uncle that a female banker would not engender the necessary respect, particularly among members of the business community. In the end, he bowed to my wishes.

(However, I cannot imagine his acquiescence had the prostitute Althea been the woman I wanted to hire. She lobbied for the position, and her adept handling of her own investments more than qualifies her for the job. Nevertheless, I am sure you can understand that her current employment disqualifies her from consideration.)

In any event, indications thus far are that Margaret (a miner's widow, childless) will prove a valuable asset to the bank. And as our clientele is becoming cognizant of that fact, she is gaining acceptance. She is also learning the subtleties of finance, and I do not doubt she will come to understand the many ways (with an adjustment here, a transfer there) that a bank can profit from the funds placed in its trust.

I see Margaret now, standing near the gallows with Lila, another local widow (the one whose farmer husband died some years ago at Harlow Mackelprang's hand, a brief account of which crime and its aftermath I related earlier). Lila cooks at the café where I take most of my meals. (The café must be closed for the hanging, as, apparently, is every other business in town.)

I would not have predicted such a level of interest. Most of the residents of Los Santos and the immediate environs appear to have turned out for the occasion.

Adults mill and talk quietly, jockeying for a favored position from which to view the event that will protect the town from violence and corruption (from one front, at least). Children are running and laughing, dodging among the more somber adults in games of tag and hide-and-seek. I wonder how the little ones will react when Harlow Mackelprang is led out to hang.

For that matter, I wonder how I will react.

I have chosen my spot so that I can get a good look at him when he passes. I wonder, should his eye catch mine, if he will acknowledge me. Perhaps I will look different to him and he will not recognize me.

Because, remember, the last time Harlow Mackelprang saw me I was covered in blood and gore.

I can't seem to get the taste of it out of my mouth.

BROOM

Harlow Mackelprang's last supper is nothing now but a few dried-up strands of sauerkraut, some gravy smears gone hard, a little piece of meat fat, and some biscuit crumbs.

His empty plate is the first thing I see in the vacant cell, sitting over there in the corner on a tray with a bowl and an empty mug and a wadded-up cloth. I suppose I'll carry that tray over to the café later, once I've cleaned up this place and the café opens back up after the hanging. Maybe there'll be a cup of coffee in it for me—which I could sure use just now to burn this fur off my tongue.

Although a drink of whiskey would do a better job, come to think of it.

All in good time. Right now I got work to do.

I drag the bucket that serves as a chamber pot out from under the cot and scrape in the leavings from the dinner plate. I haul the bucket into the walkway and carry the tray into the office, then drag the mop pail over to the cell and start in to swabbing the floor.

"Will you be cleaning my cell as well, my good man?"

I jumped a foot in the air at the question, not expecting there was anyone in the jail save me. It took a minute to focus my rheumy old eyes, but I finally got my bearings on a fat man standing down in the end cell.

"What?"

"Will my 'living area,' so to speak, be getting a cleaning?"

"Oh, no. I only do this when someone leaves. Live in your own filth until you do. I'll be along to empty your bucket, though."

"Excellent. It does get foul in here."

"How long you been locked up?"

"This is my fourth day."

"Why?"

"Why? Why what?" he asked.

"Why for are you in here?"

"A minor business dispute. A mere misunderstanding that will be cleared up posthaste once I have the opportunity to appear before the bar of justice."

"Oh," I said, and kept mopping.

"What, if I may be so bold to ask, is your name, kind sir?

What a windbag. I wonder what it would be like to be locked up in here with him for four days. About now, Harlow Mackelprang might be thinking hanging ain't such a bad thing.

"Broom," I said, and kept mopping.

"Broom." He mulled that over for a minute, then asked, "Is that your surname or given name?"

"Ain't neither. It's just what folks call me."

"Broom. Very good then. Call me Sweeney. Will you be attending this morning's execution, Broom?"

"Nope."

"It seems we will be the only ones in town not in attendance."

"Yup."

"Are you acquainted with the condemned, Broom?"

"Knowed him all his life."

"I understand there is no question of his guilt. Do you concur?"

"Mr. Sweeney, I know for a fact that Harlow Mackelprang ain't no good for nothing," I said as I wrung out the mop for the last time. "And it's my own damn fault."

Maybe for the first time in his life, Sweeney looks to be at a loss for words. I ain't going to help him find any.

Guilt ain't an easy thing for a man to live with. And I sure as hell feel guilty about Harlow Mackelprang. Who wouldn't feel that way if his own boy, his own flesh and blood, grew up to be a gunman and took up a life of thieving, raping, robbing, and killing.

Not that I taught him such things, you understand. But I never taught him different. Fact is, I don't guess I taught him much of anything at all.

I'll tell you, when the midwife finally allowed me in to see Bonnie and our newborn babe, I thought there was nothing finer in all the world. My beautiful young wife, with that red and wrinkled-up little baby snuggled up to her, plumb made my heart pound. And that glow carried me along for a good long time.

I'd come on home from a shift at the mine and

find Bonnie putting the finishing touches on my supper—or breakfast when I had the night shift. Nothing fancy, just plain food, but Bonnie had a way of making anything tempting and tasty. The place, small and run-down though it was, was always swept and polished till it sparkled and dolled up with curtains and tablecloths and such that Bonnie whipped up from out of nothing.

She always saw to it that our little shack was the best-kept-up place in Mechanicsville—not that many others in that dusty crevice cared about such things as that. It was a hard ground for a family to take root in, and the mining combinations that owned everything aboveground and below in the Meeker's Mill district never made it any easier.

But that baby made it all worthwhile for me and Bonnie. Our little boy was about the smartest one ever born, is how we thought. Why, he'd google and coo and grin near about every time you looked at him. He learned early on how to talk, and Bonnie would have him say new words to me every day, and she'd swell up with pride and tell stories about all the other smart things he'd been up to.

It was near about as perfect a life as a man could ask for in them conditions. Good home with a loving family. Steady work and wages at the mine. And prospects for more of the same for as long into the future as we could see.

I guess I should have known that nothing that good was bound to last.

When the boy was just turned three, Bonnie took sick with pneumonia. Nothing would shake it. The poor woman was racked with coughing fits that took her breath away and she could not hardly get it back.

The company doctor tried any number of cures from bromides to meal poultices to bleeding to wrapping her in a pneumonia jacket. Finally, though, she just couldn't get any more air into her and she faded away in her sleep, leaving me and the boy alone.

That's when the whiskey took ahold of me. Before then, see, I only took a drink from time to time to celebrate a special occasion. Bonnie didn't hold with liquor, and that was all right by me since I could take it or leave it and mostly left it be, even before we got hitched.

But I turned to drink when she died, thinking it would dull the ache, but it never did.

I found a local woman to help look after the boy, but she had seven or eight kids of her own. She was a trashy woman, her shack coated with dirt and grime and infested with vermin. Her kids was always skinny with snotty noses and runny eyes.

I can't say about the sniffles, but you didn't have to look far to see why them kids was skinny. That woman weighed three hundred pounds if she weighed one. I suspected them kids had to fight her for every scrap of food they got. She was filthy in her personal habits to the point that I wondered how her man, who worked with me at the mine, managed to get near enough to her to father all them kids, but it was obvious he did it somehow— leastways somebody did.

Anyhow, all my boy's brightness just sort of dimmed out. From that crowd he learned to fight for what he wanted or steal it when no one was looking, or he would not have got anything. The meanness he got there was the beginning, I hold, of all that was to come.

Myself, I was never the mean sort, drunk or sober. But now and then somebody would get to botherin' me, pushing me down when I was barely able to stand, or beating me down and stealing whatever they might find on my person. Miners are a rough lot, and when some of them get on a toot they can get downright nasty. The crowd I ran with was no worse than most, I guess, but they never showed no mercy to someone who was helpless.

When I had them over to my home to share a bottle, they usually repaid the kindness by packing off anything of value they could lay hands on while I was passed out or sleeping it off. A time or two, some of them got to roughhousing and things would get busted up.

From time to time I myself might rummage through the pockets of a man down in an alley, but I never gave no one a beating or picked on anyone as some did and never stole nothing out of someone's house, nor broke things for the hell of it. Mostly, I was a sullen and solitary drinker, more likely to be found crying than in high spirits or mean and nasty.

For two years we lived like that, me and the boy. He didn't get much care at home, I'll admit. I guess it just didn't seem so bad at the time, looking at it like I was through the fog caused by cheap whiskey.

But the worst was still to come.

One day at work, we were barring down slabs after blasting in the number-twelve stope on the eight hundred level. We were working quick, so we could get the muck out, lay in the timber, and drill another round to make a muck pile for the next shift.

See, we hadn't done the actual blasting that we were cleaning up after. The way it works is, the other shift fires the round last thing so the smoke and gas clear out during shift change. Then, when you show up in your workplace, half your day's job is waiting for you.

First, you make sure all the powder fired. Sometimes a round don't go off right, leaving unexploded powder in one or more of the holes. If you got a misfired round, you have to reset the fuses and shoot off what didn't go the first time. Leaving it is likely to get you killed.

Most times, though, the blasting goes just fine and all you have to do is check around for any loose slabs of rock and knock them down so they don't fall and mash you while you're working.

Then it's a matter of moving the muck—"muck" being the miner's term for all the dirt and rocks broke up by the blast. Of course the plan is that the muck be laced with metal-bearing ore, but sometimes you're just moving through plain old rock to get to a vein or a lead.

This stope we was working was up a short raise, just a rod or so above track level. So mucking there amounted to pushing the muck to a chute that empties down to ore cars sitting on rails in the drift. Then you push those cars out to the station and dump them so's the muck can be loaded in a skip and hauled up the shaft to the surface, where it'd be dumped in a waste pile or sent to the mill, depending.

When that's done, you pound steel to punch a pattern of holes in the next hunk of rock to be moved, load them holes with powder—generally sticks of dynamite—and last thing you do is light the fuse on the way out. Of course it's a lot more complicated than that, but all the details don't need telling here.

So, as I said before my mind wandered off, we were barring down a slab so we could get at the mucking without worrying about it hanging over us. My partner was a bohunk name of Warenski who was about as strong as an ox and only a little bit smarter. He was prying on that big hunk of rock when it split, and the end of it we figured would stay put is the one that fell.

Fell right where I was standing, as it happened.

It weren't such a big rock that it could have killed me, but on the way down it made brief stops on the back of my head, my shoulder, and finally the middle of my back as we each hit the ground about the same time. It wrenched my back something awful and I could not get up.

Warenski got some help and they strapped me to a length of laggin' to get me out. They lowered me with ropes down through the ore chute to the drift— the drop, as I said, was only fifteen, sixteen feet or so—and strapped me and my backboard to the top of an ore car and rolled me down the drift.

I tell you, I can still feel every little piece of rock on those rails and every joint in the track. Then they propped me up in the man cage, still strapped to my laggin'—which is just a plank used to wall up between timbers—and hoisted me to the surface.

After five weeks, and more bottles of whiskey than I can count, I was able to walk again. But any lifting or even bending or twisting was out of the question. Meaning, of course, that I was out of a job.

I packed up what little belongings me and the boy owned—which wasn't much by that time, me having swapped everything of any value we owned for drink; the rest of it stole by my drinking' pards for the same reason—and we boarded the train at Meeker's Mill—the end of the rail line—intending to ride it as far as we could.

Which wasn't far, as the conductor discovered right away that we had paid no fare and carried no tickets. He put us off at the next stop, which happened to be Los Santos, and here we have been for nigh onto twenty years since.

At least *I* have been here all that time, my boy Harlow Mackelprang being absent these past three years living the life of a gunman and outlaw.

Sweeney must have finally regained his powers of speech, and he jolts me back to the present with a question.

"Broom, I confess you have me at a disadvantage. How could it possibly be that you bear responsibility for the misdeeds of a hardened criminal the likes of Harlow Mackelprang?"

"Oh, it ain't so hard to figure. He's my boy."

"What?"

"My son. I'm his pa."

"Imagine that. I confess it does not enter one's mind that notorious characters such as Harlow Mackelprang even have parents. Logic, of course, says they must. But one assumes they somehow sprung into existence fully formed, complete with bad habits and lack of character. And yet you are his father."

"Not much of one. Which is probably why he turned out as bad as he did."

"Surely, man, you gave it your best effort."

"No, Sweeney, I can't say as I did."

"Your good wife then. Surely she attempted to form his character into more productive avenues."

"It started out that way, sure, you bet. But, see, his ma died when he weren't but knee-high to a grasshopper."

"A tragedy to be sure," Sweeney said. "But a man does what he can."

"A man would, sure. But not me. When my Bonnie went to her grave, I might as well have gone with her. I turned to drink and have not had the will to turn away. Then I got hurt in the mine and lost my job. Haven't had one to speak of since."

"As bad as that then, Broom?"

"Oh, hell, yes. I got no illusions anymore about what I am. God knows I'm reminded of it often enough."

"What do you mean?"

"Ask anyone about ol' Broom. They got more names for what I am than I can remember. A drunk, of course. And drunkard. Then there's 'sot' and 'boozer' and 'soak' and 'stiff' and 'lush.' Fancier names too, like 'alcoholist' and 'dipsomaniac.' They'll tell you I'm all the time soused, stewed, and swizzled. Liquored up, inebriated, on a bender, on a toot, top-heavy, tight, and tangle-footed.

"I know what I am all right. And I know it didn't do my boy Harlow Mackelprang any good having the town drunk for an old man. On top of that, I'm accused of being lazy and shiftless and not willing to work."

"Is that so? I mean, have you shunned gainful employment?"

That produced a laugh. "Working steady would interfere with my drinking, Sweeney," I say. "Can't have that, you know."

He did not reply, and my laughter soon faded. I decide to point out the irony of the situation. Which is strange in itself, all this talking on my part. I have not strung this many words together since I don't know when.

"Truth is, I don't know if I can't work because I drink too much or if I drink so much because I can't work. You remember I talked about that time I got hurt in the mine?"

"Of course."

"Well, see that really did mess up my back something awful, and it ain't got any better even after all these years. I can't lift hardly anything—even just bending over sometimes, I get stuck that way and have to lay right down for a spell until I can get straightened out. Reaching, twisting, even sitting still for more than a few minutes pains me something awful. So what kind of work is a man in my condition suited for?

"Being useless is bad enough. And hurting like hell most of the time don't help any. Drinking dulls the pain in my back some, but I don't know if it hurts or helps when it comes to the feelings that dog my mind of being a useless no-good so-and-so and no-account father of a rotten kid. Maybe it helps, maybe it makes it worse—on account of drinking sometimes makes me brood about it.

"One more thing about a bad back—it don't show. Take the marshal now. He's got a bunged-up knee so's he walks with a limp. Or you take a man who's had an arm took off, or something like that. Them injuries show. Not so when it's your back. So folks never know if you're telling the truth or just telling tales on account of you're lazy. Most people think it's laziness.

"I manage to pick up enough money to keep my bottle full by cleaning up here, swabbing out the saloon, sweeping up at the café and general store and freight office, things like that. It ain't much, but it's all I'm good for."

"A sad tale to be sure," Sweeney opines. "I cannot imagine, however, that the good people of Los Santos hold one in your difficult circumstances accountable for a wayward son's actions."

"Maybe not anymore. But early on, they didn't mind telling me about it every time he done something wrong and demanding I do something to make it right. Most times I was too drunk to care about what they said, let alone doing anything about it. It started out simple enough. I left the boy to wander the streets and folks would cuss me for being neglectful and irresponsible.

"Then, in a few years, they was always after me because he wouldn't stay in school. It got worse from there. Stealing stuff, breaking things, like that. Most times no one saw him do it, but it was pretty much the order of things around here that if something was missing or messed with, then Harlow Mackelprang must of done it. The older he got, the worse it got."

"Was there nothing you could do, Broom, to alleviate the situation?"

"Nothing that worked. Not that I tried all that much. Talking went in his one ear and out the other. The few times I took a strap to him didn't help. Most times when I did sober up enough to try to correct him, he would just run off and hide somewhere and stay hid up till I wasn't sober anymore. Even he knew I'd be falling down drunk again before too long.

"That's one thing about the kid—he ain't stupid. Mean, sure. Maybe even crazy. But from early on he was smart enough to figure out how to get what he wanted without getting caught, and to weasel his way out of trouble when he did.

"But that don't last too long in a town this small, and after a while no one was buying his act. By then it was too late anyway. He was too far gone and I was too far gone to care overmuch."

"But you do still care, don't you, Broom. I sense that the guilt affects you more than the drink—and is the harder habit to break."

"Could be, I guess. Hell, I don't know. I try not to think about it too much. Just makes me thirsty. So does talking. I ain't talked this much since I don't know when."

"Talking. Now there's something I have a talent for. The fine arts of oratory and rhetoric, combined with the ability to intuit human nature, along with a flair for persuasion have enabled me earn a fine living," Sweeney said.

"Ended you up in here, though, didn't it, all that talking."

"Every job has its hazards, Broom, every job its hazards. In mining, as in your case, the dangers are physical. In my line, they run to legal disputes and jail time. Although, on occasion, a promoter may be tarred and feathered or ridden out of town on a rail. Some have been subject to a beating or even a shooting at the hand of a disgruntled customer. But those are rare occurrences, thank goodness. Violence is not often a danger in my line of work."

This prompted another ironic laugh on my part.

"Once again, Broom, you have me at a disadvantage. Where, pray tell, is the humor in my statement?"

"Oh, I was just thinking what you said—every job having its hazards. Here you are in jail, here I am a useless drunk. But that ain't nothing compared to what my boy Harlow Mackelprang got on account of his chosen line—they'll be stretching his neck any minute now, by my reckoning."

Once more, Sweeney was at a loss for words.

"I guess I better get finished up here. I don't want to be around when that strong-arming marshal gets back. Slide your honey bucket over here by the door, then stand back out of the way. Not that I don't trust you, Sweeney, but the last thing I need is for a prisoner to escape on account of the town drunk not paying attention."

Sweeney did just that, and I unlocked the cell door and opened it just enough to slide the bucket through. Keeping one eye on him, I dumped his mess into the bucket from Harlow Mackelprang's cell and returned it empty, locking the door. Then I poured in the mop water, stood the mop in the empty mop pail, and slid them into the corner.

"I'll be going now, Sweeney. Been nice talking to you."

"The pleasure has been all mine, I assure you, Broom. The pleasure was all mine."

With that, I picked up the full bucket and left through the marshal's office. As I walked around the jailhouse to the ditch out in the back alley, I could hear the crowd over there where the gallows is.

Of a sudden, things got real quiet.

Then there was this loud bang and low twangy hum and what sounded like every man, woman, and child in Los Santos sucking in a big breath all at once, just as I dumped the remains of Harlow Mackelprang's last supper into the ditch.